CW00807412

BETH AGAIN

by

Julia Scott

Published by New Generation Publishing in 2021

First Edition

ISBN 978-1-80031-346-0

www.newgeneration-publishing.com

 New Generation Publishing

February

A radiant fingernail of moon shone brightly in an inky-black starlit sky as Beth trudged away from the hospital. Her clumpy boots crunched loudly in to the deep, crisp snow, her fingers feeling numb inside her thin gloves as she gripped the buggy handlebar. The air was dry and sharp, making her earlobes and nose-tip tingle, but the night was still so it didn't feel as bitterly cold as it might have.

Holly was snug and warm cocooned in the fleecy cave of her buggy, fast asleep and silently dreaming of …what? Beth suddenly realised that she didn't have a clue whether six-week-old babies dreamt or not. Probably not, she concluded, as they have little or no knowledge or experience to dream about, living a tiny life of purely senses, but who knew, really?

Beth felt tired deep inside, the emotional rollercoaster of the last eight weeks weighing heavily on her. Two weeks before Christmas, she'd moved whilst heavily pregnant to Lincoln, to her grandparent's home, having been rejected by her parents for refusing to have an abortion. Within days of Christmas her grandfather, already in hospital recovering from a heart attack, had suffered a major stroke and had been in a coma ever since; the last time Beth had seen him awake had been when he'd smiled in his hospital bed after opening her small gift to him on Christmas Eve night, only hours before Holly had been born. Holly's jaundice had meant Beth's own stay in the neo-natal wing of the hospital had been extended to five days, during which time Walter Gregson's stroke had taken everyone by surprise as he'd seemed stable following his minor heart attack. Now, five weeks on, Beth could only snatch short visits with him whilst her grandmother walked Holly around the hospital grounds, as new-borns were strictly forbidden from entering hospital wards.

Not only was Beth a teenaged, sleep-deprived, first-time mother, she was also totally alone apart from her grandparents, whom she hardly saw. Her grandmother, Gwen, had kept a close vigil by Walter's bedside since his stroke and only came home briefly to shower and change every other day; she had been quite round and healthy looking when Beth and Joe had arrived at her house two weeks before Christmas, but Beth could see the changes in her after too many nights on a rigid, black lazy-boy chair beside Walter and too many days surviving on sandwiches and tea. She'd refused all offers of home-cooked meals or take-aways, saying she was too anxious to eat, the result being that Beth was worried about both her grandparents. Beth kept her supplied with bananas and chocolate, but she knew that was not a long-term solution.

A light flurry of snow had begun to fall again, so the final half-mile home pushing the buggy had been hard work, but at least she could now see her gran's front room light, which she'd deliberately left on, glowing from behind the curtains, welcoming her to a warm, familiar refuge. Only two more days until Joe arrived for the weekend and she couldn't wait to see him, couldn't wait to offload some of her worries on him and couldn't wait to have someone her own age to talk to for a few days. She was desperate, no two ways about it. The next hour would be taken up feeding and changing Holly and then making herself some cheese on toast and a cup of hot chocolate, then she'd call Joe to check what time he'd be arriving; she felt excited and happy for the first time in weeks as she closed the front door behind her.

#

Gwen woke up with a stiff neck after sleeping awkwardly in the lazy-boy chair. The room was very quiet, too quiet she realised with a jolt of fear, the dim light adding to her feeling of impending doom. She struggled to get herself upright as a sharp pain shot down her neck and into her shoulder, but she was nevertheless acutely aware of the lack of gentle snoring which had been coming from Walter when she'd dozed off earlier in the evening, a quiet, purring snore that had lulled her to sleep.

She knew immediately she took his hand that he had left her, even though his flesh was still warm to the touch. Silent tears cascaded down her cheeks as she pressed the buzzer to call a nurse, who quickly confirmed his death and began gently disconnecting the various treatments which had been maintaining his life. She fetched an upright chair and placed it behind Gwen, kindly encouraging her to sit with her husband whilst she fetched a calming cup of tea.

After a few minutes, the night doctor arrived to officially record the death, all done very efficiently and almost silently as it was still the middle of the night. Gwen refused a taxi home or a phone call, saying she'd prefer to sit quietly in Walter's room with him until morning, so all the covers were removed from him to allow the body to cool. She drifted into a mindless, numb wakefulness, only roused out of that state when the early-morning tea trolley clattered past the door at 7.30am.

#

Beth was sitting at the kitchen table enjoying toast and tea when she heard the front door open and close. As she watched Gwen enter the kitchen, she could instantly see the devastation and exhaustion on her grandmother's face; she walked quietly round the table and wrapped her arms around Gwen's now slight body and held her close as she cried herself hoarse, then helped her to her bedroom and tucked her in for a long-overdue sleep.

She'd lost her appetite for her breakfast and was throwing it in the bin when she heard Holly stirring. The warmth of her baby was just what she needed and she shed her own silent tears as she buried her face in Holly's tiny body. Beth was now desperate for Joe to arrive and began willing the next forty-eight hours away; Joe was fond of Gwen and Beth felt confident his company would raise both of their spirits. She made up her mind to call him immediately she'd seen to Holly, give him a heads-up on what had happened, then she'd check on her grandmother and make sure she was still asleep.

#

Joe's family home was so small that the screaming smoke alarm on the kitchen wall was deafening, even in his bedroom, making it impossible for him to hear Beth's voice on his mobile, so he raced down the stairs to swiftly pull the batteries out of the alarm. Thin black smoke filled his nostrils and made his eyes water as he instantly became aware of the rasping, scraping noise of Martha trying to rescue blackened toast with a knife. Eggs and bacon were bubbling away in the frying pan on the hob and looked distinctly as if they needed rescuing too, but Joe was anxious to get back to what Beth was saying to him.

"Mum, what the heck's going on, the eggs are burning too and I'm on the phone," he shouted across the smog of the room.

"Damn and blast, I've burned the last two pieces of bread, ruined the eggs and bacon and now I've cut my finger on this bloody knife, what a start to the day," she cursed as she wrapped some kitchen paper around her finger and flew over to the hob to switch everything off. Joe stretched over the sink to open the window wide with one hand as he gripped his mobile tightly in his other hand and listened to Beth's tearful news, but he was lost for words.

"Are you still coming on Friday Joe, because I really need you, I don't know how to cope with all this, I don't know what to say …. or what to do …. can you please still come?"

"My ticket's already booked Beth, I'll be there by teatime, so just hang in there, you'll be fine." He sounded more sure of himself than he felt, but she needed him to be confident and strong – again. "I suppose there will be legal things to sort out, papers to sign or something – I don't know, I was too young when my grandparents died, but I'll check with Mum so don't worry. I'll help you and your gran sort it when I get there, ok?"

"OK, I'll see you the day after tomorrow then, thanks Joe," then the phone went dead.

Martha was standing stock still with her finger still bleeding into the kitchen paper, listening to this conversation and filling in the gaps she couldn't hear. Once again, she was concerned that her son was assuming too much responsibility for a lad of seventeen, worried that he'd had to grow up too early with his dad being away so much of the time throughout his and Freddy's childhoods.

"Joe, I know you've booked a ticket to go and see Beth and that it's almost half-term at school, but are you sure you're not taking on too much? It was one thing to visit with her grandfather in hospital and her gran there with him most of the time, but now he's died Joe, there'll be a lot to do: registering the death and contacting everyone who legally needs to know like the solicitor, DWP, doctor and so on, plus a funeral to organise …. are you up to it? You also have schoolwork to do, deadlines to meet with course work and so on and, much as I'm fond of Beth, she leans on you one hell of a lot and you always put yourself second Joe; don't you think it's time Beth's parents stepped up their game and took on some responsibility, rather than you?"

"Mum, you know they virtually disowned Beth when she refused to have an abortion. I don't think she or her gran have had any contact with the Gregsons since they forced

7

Beth to go and stay with her grandparents; they've shown no interest at all in their daughter or their first grandchild, other than sending some money for Christmas gifts whilst they swanned off to somewhere hot on an aeroplane. What makes you think they'll care now?"

"I don't know Joe, but they have to be given the chance, don't they? I know Beth's gran is still mentally sharp and she probably has plans in place already, but I would imagine Ray will be involved as he's their elder child and only son – is his sister even in the country?"

"I don't know Mum. Can you please go through what has to be done immediately, in case Beth's gran is too grief-stricken to focus? You've been through it twice with your parents, so you must know basically what has to happen first?"

"Yes, OK, but don't play the hero Joe, let Beth's gran do it all if she's able to, just be kind of supportive, alright?" She gave him a big hug and managed to smear blood all over his clean white T-shirt. "Oh bugger, this is not going to be a good day, is it?"

#

Molly and Ray Gregson had been home from their Christmas vacation for two weeks and Molly was mentally still in The Virgin Islands, unwilling to forget her four weeks of escapism too easily. She'd barely spared a thought for Beth or her pregnancy for the whole month away, living a selfish lie of wine, food, sea and decadence. The memory of all that was destroyed very abruptly with Gwen's phone call to Ray, telling him of his father's death, which had brought them both back to reality with an unwelcome bump.

Ray had never been particularly close to his parents, so the expectation of duty grated on him.

"Right, do you really need me to come to Lincoln, or can you handle things for now, Mother?" His unfeeling response surprised Gwen, even though she understood her son better than he knew.

"It's your father Ray, surely you can come and help with the formalities, help arrange the funeral and so on?"

"Possibly, but you have got Beth with you and can't Joyce come and help? It's just that things are not going so well at the clinic right now and I really need to be here." He sounded impatient, Gwen realised and she was hurt by his indifference.

"Joyce is on her way and will arrive from Ireland tomorrow, but he was your father too Ray, you should be here, but I can't force you," then she sadly put the phone down. Ray turned to find Molly standing behind him, listening to this difficult conversation.

"You know Ray, maybe we should go up there for a night or two, show willing, set eyes on the brat Beth has produced, listen to any last will and testament that might be read, you know?" She was studying his face, knowing that the mention of a will might just interest him, even if nothing else did.

"Mmm, you may be right, but the problems at the clinic are pretty urgent right now, I don't know if I can get away." Ray had not shared with Molly that the clinic had been closed pending a criminal medical negligence hearing, brought about by their interfering ex-GP Kate Monroe and corroborated by their ex-secretary, Sophie. As far as Molly was concerned, the clinic was shut for refurbishments due to structural problems.

"Surely you can get away for a while, you can't do much with the clinic closed, can you? It's not that I want to see your mother, you know that, but it might just be beneficial to us, if you know what I mean. Also, I want to make sure Beth knows that she's not coming back home with a baby in tow. So, Ray, think about it whilst I get some dinner on the go," then she waltzed off brightly to the kitchen, happy with her suggestions.

#

For as long as she could remember, Beth had been aware of the lack of love and affection between her dad and his mother, so it warmed her through and through to witness the closeness between her aunt Joyce and Gwen. The embrace between mother and daughter immediately Joyce had walked into the house lasted a full minute, a long time for a hug in Beth's experience; she suddenly realised she was sitting with a grin on her face as she watched the two women holding each other close.

"How are you coping Mum, you look tired and thin," Joyce said in a voice full of concern. "I hadn't realised Dad was so…. well, I just expected him to come out of the coma one day soon, that's all, or I'd have come home sooner. Is Ray here yet?"

"I'm not sure we'll see Ray at all Joyce; he has problems at the clinic and he doesn't think he can get away."

"What? It's Dad's funeral, surely he can make the effort to be here for once? That's disgraceful, selfish!"

"Well, he sounded very unwilling when I spoke to him earlier, very worried in fact, so we mustn't judge him. You sit and talk to Beth love, I'll make us all a cuppa."

"No, Gran, I'll make the tea, you sit with aunty Joyce for a bit," then she got up to kiss her aunt before heading off into the kitchen. Beth could hear her gran explaining all that had been going on since Christmas with Walter's decline, she could hear Joyce's soothing words when Gwen began to cry again and she also felt for herself the adult support that Joyce had brought in to the house. No longer was Beth the only person her gran was leaning on and the sudden sense of relief surprised her.

"Tea up people, I've cut three slices of your new fruit cake too Gran, I hope that's ok." The three of them spent the next half hour catching up on all the news, Beth's secret pregnancy and the details about Holly's birth in a locked church very early on Christmas morning, which had them all laughing hysterically – emotional reaction to grief, for sure.

"Well, that'll be one story to bring up on Holly's wedding day won't it, Beth – you'll dine out on that one for years to come," Joyce said as she wiped the laughter tears from her eyes. "I bet Dad smiled at that story too, didn't he Mum?"

"He did, he really did," Gwen said as she pushed cake crumbs around her plate with her index finger, lost in a recent happy memory. "Now, come on Joyce, let's get you unpacked and settled in. You're in your old box room, I hope you don't mind, but Beth's in Ray's old bedroom with the cot and everything for Holly.

"I'll be just fine in my old bed Mum, just like old times again," then she disappeared out of the room pulling her heavy suitcase behind her. "I'll just have a freshen up in the bathroom, then I'll go and get us all some fish and chips, how does that sound? My bloody selfish brother doesn't know what he's missing, does he Beth?" she called as she headed down the hallway.

#

Joe arrived at teatime the next day and Beth was at the bus station to greet him as he jumped off the bus with a backpack slung over one shoulder, landing in a great bear-hug, which squeezed the breath out of her. It felt good to hold her close and, being honest with himself, he realised how much he really didn't want to let go of her.

"Let go Joe, I can't breathe," she squealed with delight as she grinned up at him. "I'm so glad you're here, I've been looking forward to you coming for days."

"It's been really hard for you, I know, but I'm here now for a few days, so lighten up."

"It has been hard, really hard, but it's much better now that aunty Joyce has arrived. She's great, I really like her and she's organising everything, but I don't remember her much from when I was a kid – think I only saw her a couple of times in all my childhood. Anyway, she's watching Holly for me for a couple of hours, so we can go for a walk or a sandwich or something, whatever you like."

"Oh right, am I sleeping on the sofa again then?", he said with a laugh. "Good job I left my sleeping bag here last time, eh? I'm starving, let's walk down to that café in the park and you can tell me what's been happening." They hadn't gone more than three steps before he took hold of her hand and they headed off towards the park smiling happily.

#

One week later, Joyce answered a very impatient and persistent ringing on the doorbell to find Ray and Molly staring her in the face.

"Well, not before time, eh Ray? Mum will be thrilled to see you."

"Nice to see you too Joyce and no doubt you've got everything organised and in hand, so don't try to make me feel guilty, right?" The two of them stepped into the narrow hallway and waited for Gwen to come out of the kitchen, where they could hear her pottering about.

"Hello love, I'm so glad you decided to come after all, it was the right decision. How are you both, did you have a good holiday?"

"We're fine Mum and yes, we had a nice break away." Ray leaned forward and gave Gwen a lightning quick kiss on the cheek, followed by a cursory nod towards Joyce. Molly then stepped forward and repeated both gestures, formal and cool as ever.

"We can't stay long right now Gwen, we need to go and check in at the hotel in town and then we'll get some dinner somewhere, won't we Ray. I think it's best if we come around tomorrow morning, after breakfast, what do you think?" Molly was too busy brushing some fluff off her sleeve to look Gwen in the face, but Ray nodded his agreement and they turned to leave almost immediately.

"Hang on a minute, aren't you going to say hello to Beth before you leave, she's just changing Holly in the bedroom?" Gwen was appalled that they hadn't given their daughter a moment's thought, nor their granddaughter.

"No, not if she's busy, we'll see her in the morning," then they left the house having only stepped in two minutes earlier.

"Un-be-lieve-able!" was Joyce's incredulous reaction, as they disappeared down the garden path and climbed into their car. "They can't even be bothered with their only daughter, whom they haven't seen for two months. Poor Beth, she's going to be upset by this."

"Upset by what?" Beth said as she came into the hall.

"I'm sorry love, that was your parents arriving and leaving again in seconds," Gwen said as she turned to see the betrayal on Beth's face. "They had to go and check in at their hotel, they'll be back tomorrow and see you and Holly then."

"You don't need to make excuses for them Gran, I know they're ashamed of me and completely uninterested in Holly. I've known that since they sent me away to you, but I'm thankful they did; it would have been miserable and impossibly difficult if I'd stayed at home. They would probably have tried to make me give Holly up for adoption or something." Beth was trying to be strong, but the hurt she was feeling was hard to disguise.

Joyce put her arm around Beth's shoulder and led her back to the sitting room.

"They do not know how lucky they are to have you as a daughter Beth, they really don't. You are an amazing young woman and I wish you were my daughter, but I wasn't so lucky. Now, let me have a cuddle with your beautiful baby, whilst you go and make the three of us a cuppa, there's a good girl." As Beth left the room, Joyce looked her mother in the eyes and silently shook her head.

#

Beth lay in her bed and watched the sun gradually lighten the early morning sky, through the narrow gap in the heavy blackout curtains which used to be her father's thirty years before, when he was roughly her age. Sleep had been her enemy throughout the entire night, a hard-fought battle which she had wrestled with for nine hours. Even after several months away from them, her parents still had the ability to completely unsettle her without her even having spoken to them, simply by ignoring her existence.

Outside it was overcast and dull, but thankfully it wasn't raining, so there was at least the promise of an outing later in the day. The silence of the house was gently broken by the snuffles and grunts of a slowly awakening hungry baby; Holly would be ravenous within minutes, so Beth got up to go and make up a bottle of formula, before her gran and Joyce were disturbed. With any luck, she could feed her baby and get her settled again for another hour or so, before she had to muster the energy to face another day and the prospect of confronting her parents.

As she tiptoed to the kitchen, she was surprised to see a light through the narrowly open door. Joyce was already nursing a cup of tea, slumped at the table and swaddled in a deep, fluffy dressing gown, looking as though she'd had no sleep either.

"There's hot water in the kettle, should be enough for Holly's bottle as well as a cuppa for you Beth, but I won't offer to do it for you, I'm shattered."

"You look like I feel aunty Joyce, I'm guessing you've been awake all night too, have you?"

"Yep, thanks to that arsehole of a brother of mine. I've spent half the night wondering how my lovely parents ended up with a selfish son-of-a-whatsit like him and the other half wondering how he and my *lovely* sister-in-law managed to rear a great girl like you. It just doesn't make any sense, there is sometimes no rhyme or reason to life. Sorry, a bit heavy for this time in the morning love, come and sit with me when Holly's back down in her crib and we'll discuss how to be civil to them in a few hours, see if we can work out some sort of miracle plan."

An hour later, nursing a second cup of tea each and wondering what the day held in store for them, they both jumped at the sudden loud ringing of the telephone. Beth watched her aunt struggle to get up and go to the hall table.

"Hello Joyce, I think it would be best if you two came to the hotel for coffee mid-morning, instead of us all cramming in to that small sitting room; neutral territory might just keep things calm, whereas your obvious annoyance with me yesterday might bubble up into something……..something unpleasant, if we're cooped up together. Molly's going shopping but should be back in an hour, so call me when you're on your way and I'll order coffee and cake for the four of us."

"What do you mean, *four of us* Ray? We will be five plus the baby," Joyce responded with instant irritation.

"Beth doesn't need to come does she, plus the baby might interrupt our discussions."

"You can't be serious Ray, what sort of heartless excuse for a human being are you? You haven't seen Beth for months and the baby never and I for one will not be the one to upset her by saying you don't want to see her, so deal with it. I'll call you when we leave." This day was going to be a real test for all of them, that was obvious.

#

The restaurant at the hotel where Ray and Molly were staying was enormous, more of a conservatory, surrounded on three sides by floor to ceiling glass and overlooking an enormous, beautifully groomed garden. The roof was frosted glass with both electric fans and heaters suspended at intervals along the length of a central support bar; it would be a couple of months before the fans were needed, but the heaters added a cosy warmth to the otherwise bright, cool, February room. The furniture was all high-quality wicker with extremely plush cushions on each seat and glass topped tables, each with a bowl of pink hyacinths in the centre. The achieved atmosphere was of relaxed, friendly optimism, which was the polar-opposite to everything each of the five adult members of the Gregson family was feeling when they sat down later that morning.

Ray and Molly were annoyed at having to be in Lincoln at all, but the hope that a generous injection of cash would be theirs after the reading of the will was enough to ensure their presence. They were not enthusiastic about seeing Beth or Holly either.

Joyce was furious with her brother; he was the elder and should have assumed more responsibility after Walter's death, should care more about Gwen's well-being, should show more concern for his daughter and first grandchild, should *care* full stop.

Gwen was grieving deeply, was disappointed in her son's obvious *lack* of grief or interest in either her or the funeral arrangements, but was particularly devastated by his rejection of Beth and the baby. What had she failed to do as a mother, to have him turn out like this? Should she feel some guilt, or could she forgive herself because Joyce had received the same upbringing yet had become a loving adult? She tortured herself over this during her sleepless nights.

Beth was afraid. She had only had brief telephone conversations with her parents during the last three months, since they sent her packing after her refusal to have an abortion and, consequently, she questioned whether they ever really wanted her or loved her in the first place. Beth realised, now that she had such powerful love for her own daughter, that her parents were lacking something fundamental and she could not envisage ever rejecting Holly, whatever mistakes she made.

The only happy Gregson was Holly, who slept contentedly in her buggy without a care in the world, whilst the others settled themselves around a vast table, a discreet distance from any other hotel guests.

#

Molly was the first to speak, as she raised her eyebrows and looked at Beth opposite her, making no attempt to look at the baby. Her expression was impossible to interpret, Beth realised; was it hostility, guilt, dislike, anger, impatience, or a combination of them all? Her tone was hard and unfeeling.

"Are you alright Beth? Have you decided whether or when you're coming back home …. *alone*? You've had twelve of the eighteen weeks of maternity leave you're allowed off school – I had a letter from your headmaster telling me to contact the School Aged Parent Team to discuss it. If you worked hard you could catch up what you've missed and return to school after Easter. In two years you could go to university, have some prospect of a career, a future."

"I have more than just myself to consider now though, don't I Mum. *I* can't be separated from *my* daughter, even if you can be separated from yours." Beth was surprised by how sure of herself she sounded, when she was feeling distinctly wobbly inside.

"What *are* you going to do then, what exactly are your plans? You know you have to stay in some sort of education until you're eighteen." Molly felt stung by Beth's response, when she'd consistently sent money every month to ease the financial burden on Gwen, even though she had made it clear from the start that she was willing to resume normal life as long as Beth had an abortion, but had been ignored. "You can't stay here with Gwen forever."

"Yes, she can," came the firm but gentle interruption by Gwen, "she can stay for as long as she needs to, for as long as it takes to decide where her future lies. No rush darling," she said as she turned and patted Beth's knee. Beth smiled gratefully and put her hand on top of Gwen's.

"Of course there's a rush Gwen, don't be so naiive; Ray and I don't want any grief from the school or anyone else just because she's not attending lessons. If you're not coming home and going back to school Beth, you'll have to look in to registering with a local school ….…..if they'll take you!" What with Holly's birth, followed by Walter's illness and death, they'd all forgotten about the legal need to continue Beth's education. "Right then, I've said my piece, I've offered to take you back, you ungrateful little……..it's up to you now, you sort it." Silence, no-one said another word for a good twenty seconds, which seemed a whole lot longer.

"Right!" All eyes turned to Ray as he clearly decided to move the conversation on. "What still needs to be done regarding the funeral, the wake, legal documents, Dad's clothes, money, the solicitor's?" At that exact moment, a waitress arrived with a pot of tea, a pot of coffee and a plate of small cakes, which she arranged in the centre of the glass table.

A second waitress arrived with a small tray holding two stacks of cups and a pile of saucers, which she set down in front of Joyce, who began to put cups on saucers and hand them out as she spoke, so that everyone could pour their own drink.

"Well, Mum, Beth and I have organised the funeral service and the flowers, but you can sort out and read the eulogy, if you want to. We thought we'd just order a platter or two of sandwiches and a few large cakes from the Bluebell Café on the High Street and have the gathering at

Mum's, unless you have any objections to that – there aren't going to be too many people at the funeral, we've kept it small. We've registered the death, obviously and we've contacted the DWP, so his pension is being stopped. Mum doesn't want to sort his clothes yet, we can do that later." She sat back and waited for his response as she tucked into a mini jam doughnut.

"You're so organised that I wonder why I needed to come at all. I knew you'd have it all in hand Joyce, you've always ruled the roost, ever since we were kids."

"Well, what a good job I am organised, because Dad would still be lying cold in the hospital mortuary if we'd waited for you to sort things …. sorry Mum," as she looked sadly towards Gwen. "You didn't come and see him when he was ill, you haven't been home here for several years, so don't criticise me for getting on with things." Joyce privately conceded that her brother had been right to have this meeting at his hotel, because her voice would definitely have been decibels higher if they'd been at home, which would have upset Gwen hugely. "Now let's behave like the adults we are and be civil with each other," then she took a great gulp of tea to calm herself.

"At least Dad didn't linger for months in the coma, brain dead on life-support; that would have been a nightmare, trying to sort euthanasia or assisted suicide, whatever. I know it's hard Mum, but I wouldn't have tolerated him being the living dead for months on end, it just prolongs the agony for everyone." Gwen was shocked by his words, unnecessary and uncalled for as they were, leaving her unable to speak. Joyce was on it though, like a flash.

"Two things Ray: first, that would *not* have been your decision, it would have been Mum's. Second, if Dad *had* been lingering, you'd have had to batter me to death before I let you end his life prematurely. Now, let's not allow this time to sink further into recriminations; we need to focus on Mum and what else needs to be done."

"What about the solicitor, the money? Is there enough to pay for the funeral? Is there a will to be read and, if so, when?" Aha, now we're getting to his real interest, Joyce pondered as she reached for her second piece of sweet comfort food, a slice of marble cake.

#

Walter's funeral was a very quiet affair, just a handful of friends and neighbours with the few family members. Barely four rows of seats were occupied in the crematorium chapel and the service was done and dusted in less than twenty minutes. Beth held Holly close throughout the short service, not worrying about the burps, burbles and other gentle baby noises she was making, thankful for the audible signs of new life during such a sad occasion.

The small gathering in Gwen's living room afterwards only lasted a couple of hours, two platters of sandwiches, two large cakes and endless pots of tea polished off completely. It was a relief to the family when the last guests drifted off and they could abandon the false smiles and forced jollity of any and every wake. Ray and Molly left soon afterwards, as Molly said she was developing one of her migraines. Gwen collapsed on to the sofa and promptly dozed off, whilst Beth disappeared to bath and feed Holly. Joyce and Joe set about tidying up the plates, cups and general mess left by any gathering, then Joyce fetched a bottle of red wine from the cupboard in the kitchen and poured them both a glass, as Joe sat at the table watching.

"How long are you planning to stay Joe? Don't you have to be back at school tomorrow?" Joyce plonked herself opposite him and took a long sip of her wine.

"I should be back, strictly speaking, but I've asked for a few days off for a family funeral, even though Walter wasn't my grandfather, but school doesn't know that. Also, as a sixth former, the Head of Year trusts me to follow the missed lessons online and make up the lost work, so I'll have to do that when I get back. How about you, are you staying long?"

"Well, as I'm single and self-employed I can stay as long as Mum needs me in theory - thank goodness for the internet eh? However, as a literary agent, I will have to get back to Dublin fairly soon as I have authors to meet with and so on, so can't stay indefinitely. I had thought maybe Mum would come back with me for a while, but she won't want to leave Beth all alone here and I don't have room for them both plus Holly in my flat. We'll see, don't need to decide now and Mum probably won't want to leave home so soon after losing Pops anyway." Joyce took another slurp of wine and reached for another glass as Beth walked in to get a bottle of milk ready for Holly. "Fancy a glass Beth, you're not breast feeding after all?"

"Why not, I haven't had any since before I knew I was pregnant, but I'll probably be drunk after half a glass, so may-be I'll have it with soda if there is any? If not, then lemonade, thanks." Five minutes later, the three of them sat sipping their drinks quietly, completely absorbed watching Holly guzzle her bottle of formula hungrily.

#

The following afternoon Gwen, Joyce, Ray and Molly arrived at Grundy and Grundy Solicitors, in the centre of town. The office was huge and oppressively traditional, with heavy mahogany shelving all along one wall, crammed with books and old-fashioned folders, matched by a vast mahogany desk, completely clear apart from one pen and a folder with 'Walter George Gregson' written on the front. Old Mr Grundy waited until the family was seated before removing Walter's will from the folder.

"Mrs Gregson," came a croaky voice from the white-haired man sitting opposite the four of them, "You will remember coming with your husband to see me barely a year ago. I think there can be little doubt that you know the contents of your late husband's will, but I am legally bound to read it out in the presence of your family. So,

'To my wife, Gwendolen Maude, I leave our home and all the contents therein, my car and all remaining monies in our bank accounts, all of which are jointly owned by us. I also leave to my wife all stocks and shares owned by me alone and the sum of £25,000 in my private pension savings account, details of which are with Grundy and Grundy Solicitors.

To my son, Raymond George, I leave my war medals and my gold watch, a gift from my parents for my 21st birthday.

To my daughter, Joyce Elaine, I leave my mother's gold locket and diamond engagement ring.

Should my wife predecease me, I leave everything, as detailed above, to my daughter Joyce Elaine, apart from the items bequeathed to Raymond George, as detailed above. Signed, Walter George Gregson. 15th day of June, 2019.'

"So, there you have it, all very straightforward. I know I can leave you, Mrs Gregson, to dispose of your husband's belongings according to his wishes and I suggest that you make an appointment, at your convenience, to compose a new will of your own, as an independent woman;" he then sat back in his oversized brown leather chair, rested both dried and mottled hands on the desk and waited for some acknowledgement that he'd finished speaking.

The sound of Ray's chair scraping on the parquet floor as he stood up abruptly took them all by surprise. He turned and left the room without speaking or making eye-contact with anyone, swiftly followed by Molly, who muttered a half-hearted 'thankyou' before disappearing.

Back in his car, parked in a nearby multi-storey car park, Ray could not contain his frustration and anger. As Molly climbed into the front passenger seat, he slammed both hands down hard on the steering wheel and made her jump.

"Whoa, steady on Ray, that's quite a strong reaction. I know you were hoping for a financial handout and it's disappointing, but you seem more annoyed than I would have expected."

"You don't understand Molly," he yelled at her in desperation. She was acutely aware of his clenched fists, the taut skin over white knuckles showing how angry he was. "I didn't just *want* some money, we desperately *need* some money; we're going under, do you hear, going under."

"Wait, whatever do you mean, *going under*? We have the clinic, which will be up and running again as soon as the refurbishments are completed, then things will be back to normal, won't they?" She was frightened by what he was saying, for the first time beginning to sense real trouble.

"Oh, for goodness sake Molly, open your eyes. You're so bloody naiive sometimes." His voice was getting louder, exasperation breaking through and he began thumping down hard on the steering wheel column. "The clinic isn't shut temporarily for refurbishments, that was just a lie to keep you from losing it and adding to my problems. The clinic is shut pending a medical negligence investigation following a complaint made by that bitch, Kate Monroe and we could be facing legal charges, a court case, maybe even lose the clinic altogether. Don't you see, we needed some money to tide us over, buy us some time, pay for legal representation in court, whatever." Tears of anger and frustration escaped and blurred his vision; he pressed his fingers to his temples and momentarily squeezed his eyes shut, trying to block out the reality of their situation, then jerked his head up and stared wildly and unseeingly out through the windscreen. "All I got was a sodding watch and some motheaten old medals; I'm his son, for God's sake, you'd think I'd get more than that, wouldn't you?" Molly sat open mouthed in disbelief, literally speechless for the first time in years. After doing an impression of a goldfish for a few moments she spluttered:

"But …… insurance, what about insurance?"

#

"You put the kettle on love, I'll go and look out those medals and the watch, in case Ray comes to fetch them; I'll get your locket and ring too whilst I'm at it."

"No rush Mum, really, I'm not leaving any time soon and I don't honestly think you'll see Ray and Molly again this visit, so just go and relax with Beth and Joe for a bit." Joyce gave her mum a quick hug before she turned to reach for the kettle.

"I heard what aunty Joyce said, have Dad and Mum left already? Have they gone home?" Beth was shocked by the realisation that she felt disappointed, she thought she'd become immune to further hurt from her parents. Gwen flopped on to the sofa beside Beth and took her hand, squeezing it hard. Joe, sitting opposite, could hardly believe that parents could be so selfish and was reminded once again how fortunate he was to have the parents he had.

"I'm not sure love, they left the meeting pretty quickly without saying anything. I don't think you should count on seeing them again, really, not this time."

"But .... but ... they didn't really meet Holly, didn't even really look at her or anything, not once. She's beautiful, she's their granddaughter, why can't they see that and be pleased? I truly thought they'd change their attitude when they saw her for the first time." She was becoming hysterical, her voice getting louder and higher; Joe watched as fat tears trickled down her face, then she screwed up her eyes and let out a cry of exasperation. Gwen felt Beth's disappointment in Ray and Molly as keenly as her own disappointment in them. Before leaving the room, Joe gently lifted a sleeping Holly from her crib and placed her on Beth's lap, where she continued to snooze peacefully in her mother's arms despite the scream, whilst silent teardrops made little damp circles on her babygro.

#

As Joe walked into the large, bright foyer of the hotel, he saw Ray and Molly signing out at the reception desk. The thunderous expression on Ray's face when he turned around and saw Joe told him this wouldn't be a fond farewell, but Joe was ready for them, consumed with anger.

"What about Beth, why haven't you come to say goodbye to her?"

"Oh, shove off, get out of my way," came the impatient reply as Ray pushed past him. Joe nipped around in front of them, they were not going to get away with this so easily and he blocked their path.

"I asked you a question, why haven't you come to say goodbye to her? She's your daughter, your flesh and blood, yet you don't seem to give a shit. What's wrong with you?" Ray pushed him hard and he fell backwards over their suitcase.

"Go home little boy, just get out of my way," then they stormed out, leaving Joe to scramble to his feet and explain away the disruption to the security guard.

MARCH

The bare, spidery thin branches reached out over the lake, like witch's fingers reaching to grasp whatever unfortunate creature came too close. Most of the trees were still without any greenery, it was still too cold for spring to make any obvious appearance, but Beth and Joe loved walking through the country park, either pushing Holly in her buggy or just by themselves, if Joyce was free to babysit for an hour or so. Today they were alone together for the first time in four weeks, since Joe had left two days after Walter's funeral; Joe had surprised Beth by turning up on the doorstep the day before, having scrounged a lift to Lincoln with his dad, who was en-route to the ferry in Hull in his lorry.

Walking further around the large, glass-clear lake, disturbed only by a few ducks causing gentle ripples to radiate outwards, they were delighted to discover the first signs that the season was changing. Delicate white and pink blossom sat gently on the slim, snarly brown branches of a few trees, like snowflakes on eyelashes, adding a delicate beauty and colour to the world that lifted their spirits. These would all but disappear in a couple of weeks, once the usual winds and rains of March and April took hold, but for now they held a transient beauty and sign of new life that made Beth take a deep and meaningful breath, then take out her mobile and snap off a few photos.

"Joe I really love spring, all the new beginnings, ducklings, bird's nests, daffodils, they're all so beautiful, so fresh and alive. It's just what we need to see right now, missing Grandpa like we all do."

"I know, it's great here, away from the traffic. Just think, this time last year life was so different: you weren't even pregnant yet, we were both studying for our G.C.S.Es, suffering old 'Fatkins' teaching us about relationships and putting condoms on bananas at school, then the exams, hard to believe so much has changed, for you mostly. Do you miss what you had back then, living with your crappy parents, but having no worries other than school assignments?"

Beth pondered this question for quite a while as they walked on, watching the ducks.

"I suppose, really, that the pressure of study and looming exams seemed huge this time last year, but it doesn't compare with the responsibility I have now as a mum of a three-month-old. I didn't realise how much freedom I had in one way, no-one to worry about other than myself." She paused for a few steps, then "I didn't realise what I was missing out on though, because I'd never had the sort of home life that you have with your parents. I think my parents are missing a gene or something, they just don't know, have never known, *how* to love me and, now that I have Holly, I realise that there's something seriously lacking in them. I know I wouldn't be without Holly now, she's my life, so how did they never love me that way? I guess I'll never know because I can't talk to them, just can't communicate with them properly. Gran is great though, I'm really happy here with her, apart from not seeing you all the time, like I used to."

"I'm sure they love you in their own way, just different from my folks, but I know what you mean. I could never put my finger on why your home was so different from mine – I thought it was just that your parents had more money, smarter home, all that stuff, but I was wrong; it's the relationships I have that were not present in your home." Beth walked on in silence for a few steps, then closed off the negative thoughts of the previous ten minutes.

"Whatever, enough, I don't want to think about it now; hey, look over there, at that swan." As Joe turned to follow where she was pointing, she gave him a huge nudge, pretending to push him in to the water, just like old times. "Hah, got you, race you to the café," and she sprinted off, leaving him to regain his balance and grinning from ear to ear.

#

Joyce was walking around the living room with Holly hoisted on to her shoulder, firmly rubbing her small back and listening for a trapped burp or two to materialise. Gwen was on the sofa with a ball of wool and knitting needles, trying to remember how to knit a cardigan for Holly like the numerous ones she did for Beth sixteen years before. The knuckles on her hands were swollen and stiff and she struggled to even cast on the first few stitches, but she stubbornly kept going whilst Joyce watched her every move.

"Mum, do you want to swap, you burp Holly and I'll cast on for you?"

"No, it's ok love, I want to do this. Use it or lose it, they say, so I need to keep using it." Joyce really looked at her mum objectively for the first time in weeks and noticed how thin she'd become, even more-so than before the funeral.

"Mum, you're looking very thin, we need to get some more meat on your bones. Do you feel alright? How about a cuppa and a large slice of that cheesecake in the fridge?"

"A cuppa would be lovely, but my appetite hasn't really come back since Christmas, not sure why, just grief probably. I miss him you know, a lot."

"I know Mum, but you need to get some strength back, we don't want you getting ill. Here, you take Holly and I'll go and get us a snack – how about some crackers and cheese, yes?" Whilst Joyce compared her mum's tiny waist to the unmistakeable spare tyre she herself was gaining around her midriff since returning to Lincoln, Gwen nodded and smiled and settled into a cosy cuddle with Holly on the sofa.

#

Ray Gregson was sitting in a pub in the centre of town, waiting for another large whisky to follow the six he'd already necked, the last two empty glasses still sitting redundantly in front of him amid sticky, old beer mats. He'd been propping up the bar since mid-afternoon, despondently brooding over the wreckage of his business venture and the financial ruin he was now facing.

Three months earlier, before Christmas, his clinic had lost the potentially lucrative contract with a research centre in Switzerland; his abortion clinic had been providing fresh 'material' en-masse for stem cell research into life-limiting and terminal illnesses, but his business partner had bailed on him the minute their questionable practice of sponsoring students in return for these materials had faced a legal challenge. That legal challenge had come from a student, who had endured serious complications following a termination at the clinic, together with the overbearing and interfering GP whom she'd visited initially, in the days following the abortion. Consequently, the medical tribunal he'd faced earlier in the week, followed by the medical malpractice charge he'd now been found guilty of, meant the General Medical Council had revoked his right to practice any kind of medicine again. His clinic had been shut down and he'd only narrowly avoided a prison sentence, thanks only to the fact that the student had survived the ordeal, which meant he'd avoided a manslaughter charge. He was ruined. The legal costs of the case and the monetary damages awarded to the student would possibly necessitate selling both the clinic and his home too, to meet the payments. How could he face Molly, face the tirade of her anger, face losing their beautiful home and lifestyle? What should he do, where could he go? Home was not an option just now. No, he'd have another whisky and another and wait for oblivion.

Two hours and another half a bottle of whisky later, slumped in a booth to one side of the large room, Ray blurredly noticed a familiar face walk into the restaurant area beyond the bar. Kate Monroe, the GP who had initiated the medical malpractice charges against him in the first place, accompanied by a larger-than-life man with a sandy beard and slightly too long hair. He fixated his eyes on the pair and watched as they were shown to a table near the window, directly opposite him.

As he stared, he felt bile rising in his gut and pure hatred manifesting itself in his mind; *she* was responsible for the trouble he was in; *she* was the reason he was facing losing his home and his livelihood; *she* was the reason his reputation was in tatters and *she* was the reason he was now estranged from his daughter, because she hadn't arranged Beth's abortion immediately the pregnancy was discovered. How *dare* she sit there enjoying herself whilst his life was falling apart. No, justice would have to be served, right now.

Ray stood to cross the room, but found he had to grab hold of the table-top to steady himself, knocking over the remaining glass of whisky in the effort. The sound of shattering glass as the tumbler hit the tiled floor drew the attention of everyone in the building, all observers now watching to check that this clearly drunk man was not heading in their direction. Kate and Wilf briefly looked over at the kerfuffle, but Kate didn't notice that it was being caused by someone she actually knew, as waiters rushed to clear up the debris. Ray was slurring and gruffly apologised to the staff, then quickly refocussed on the couple opposite him and began to make his way unsteadily towards them.

Kate and Wilf were sipping wine and contemplating their menus as Ray stumbled over towards their table. He came to a halt only inches away and waited for them to look up at him, pleased that he'd taken them by surprise.

"Oh, Mr Gregson," Kate managed to garble out, unsure of what to expect next. "Wilf, this is Ray Gregson, the owner of the S.K.I.L.L. Clinic," she continued, as she tried to alert her husband to the impending threat. Wilf stood up, unsure of whether the gesture was from good manners or to prepare for an attack of some sort, but it was not an option to remain lower and therefor more vulnerable. On standing, he was reassured by the fact that he was not only a good deal larger than Ray Gregson but also steady on his feet in comparison, but instinct fell short of offering his hand up for a greeting.

"You can keep your *oh, Mr Gregson* and shove it up your arse. You think you can sit there an'enjoy life when you have shingle-handledly fucked up my life, do you? You have no conscience that you have shut down a rep'table abortion clinic from the community, brought fina..fina..financial ruin on me and Molly and dishtroyed any chance that Beth, a girl you *shupposhedly* cared about, might have come home. Well done you, all in a good day's work for a two-bit GP like you, you bitch."

"That's enough! I think you should go!" Wilf stepped in between Ray and Kate as he simultaneously took hold of the smaller man's arm and tried to steer him away from their table, but Ray was having none of it.

"Let go of me," Ray growled as he shook his arm free, "I'm not done with your wife yet," as he grabbed one of the glasses on the table and tossed the wine into Kate's face. Kate recoiled backwards in stunned silence as red wine dripped off her nose and chin and seeped into her white blouse, whilst the wine glass was violently smashed on the table in front of her by Ray; he then instantly scooped up all the broken fragments in both hands, which cut viciously into his flesh and threw them at her, showering her with tiny splinters of glass. Wilf instantly stepped in more forcefully and manhandled Ray away from Kate and their table, just as the bar manager and a waiter arrived at their side. Kate was handed a towel to attempt to dry herself.

"Would you come with me please sir?" came a surprisingly quiet voice as Ray tried to pull away, but the two men grasped an arm each and escorted him, still struggling, to a side room. The manager quickly reappeared with a waiter intent on clearing up the mess, then he tried to encourage Kate and Wilf to a fresh table in a different area, but they both just wanted to leave. As they gathered their jackets and left the building, they noticed Ray being 'helped' into a police car and being driven away.

#

Half an hour later, Kate noticed her hands were still trembling as she stepped out of the shower and wrapped herself in the comfort of an oversized fluffy bathrobe. She had numerous tiny marks on her neck and chest where slivers of shattered glass had cut into her on impact, but her blouse and trousers had protected her from further physical injury. The mental impact of what had just occurred left her upset and in shock though, as she grappled to get her head around those few traumatic minutes and the time since. Wilf had asked her if she'd wanted to follow to the police station and make a formal complaint, but she'd declined, she just wanted to get home. He'd pointed out that the police might want some photographs of her injuries and the state she was in, plus a statement in case she changed her mind, but she'd refused. Her thoughts were dominated by what Ray had said to her, about the repercussions on Beth long-term, but she had no sympathies with Ray himself, he deserved all he got from the tribunal.

Wandering downstairs, still swaddled in the bathrobe and with her head wrapped in a towel, Kate sat quietly at the kitchen table as Wilf plonked a bowl of steaming chicken soup in front of her.

"Not quite the sumptuous dinner we had planned, I know, but you need to eat something comforting and calming love, so tuck in." He kissed her on the top of her towelled head and squeezed her shoulder before sitting opposite her with his own soup and silently mulling over the experience they'd just had. Several minutes passed before Kate spoke.

"Why is it that men in general will always blame someone else for their mistakes? Why can men never see beyond the end of their own noses?"

"Whoa, that's a *huge* and very unfair generalisation Kate, where's this suddenly coming from? Nice to know you have such a high opinion of your husband, who's just gone to great lengths to open a tin of soup and heat it in the microwave for you – such culinary expertise." His slight sense of offence was weakly masked in a joke.

"Not you silly, of course not you. You must admit though, it's a male tendency to *not* accept responsibility for mistakes, to look for an alternative culprit if possible, rather than lose face and apologise and just move on. We *all* make mistakes, so why not just admit to them and learn from them? I mean, Ray Gregson brought all his problems on himself, didn't he? *He* decided to chase the possible lucrative rewards of successful stem cell research and followed a legally and morally appalling path to get there, virtually *paying* students to get pregnant and then terminate; he endangered lives Wilf, willingly and knowingly, yet he's chosen tonight to blame *me* for the results of those bad decisions – I rest my case!" Wilf could see the level of distress in her rising and attempted to calm her down.

"Kate, you did the right thing in reporting him and his bad practices. You saved that student's life and therefore indirectly kept Ray Gregson out of prison, you've got nothing to reproach yourself for - even where Beth is concerned – her own father changed her fortunes, not you, she's just an unfortunate victim of the fallout. Now, try to stop thinking about it, eat your soup whilst it's still warm and I'll get us both a glass of wine, because we both need to unwind now; so, red, white or rosé?"

#

APRIL

Old Mr Grundy had been sitting with Gwen and Joyce for half an hour, discussing the unusual details of Gwen's requests regarding her new will. He was an old-fashioned solicitor approaching eighty years of age, with a full head of crisp white hair and a trim moustache to match. His speech was unhurried, like his actions; he was ponderous and meticulous over every detail, but his reputation was widely known and Gwen had always trusted him.

"Mrs Gregson, it is unusual to totally exclude the elder offspring and leave the bulk of the estate to an underage grand-daughter, without causing difficulties for the young lady concerned who might, in due course, have to contend with a legal challenge from her father. Are you sure that you've thought this through?"

"Mr Grundy, Beth's father is a wealthy man with his own successful business who does not need the modest proceeds of my estate. He has shown little or no concern for his father, for me or for his sister here for some years, or even for his own daughter, from whom he is estranged. If anything should happen to me Ray would, I'm afraid, think only of himself and leave Beth out in the cold, so to speak, unless she conformed to his demands. I must protect her future if I can."

"I do understand Mrs Gregson, but it is not quite that simple. It is not legal for an underage person to inherit a house lock, stock and barrel; there would have to be a guardian and executor of your will, someone willing to take responsibility for the house until such time that Beth could legally take ownership. Do you understand?"

"Yes, I do and my daughter is willing to fill that role, aren't you Joyce?" Gwen turned and placed her hand gently on top of Joyce's, waiting for her to confirm the plan. "Also, as I'm legally handing Power of Attorney to her over my financial affairs, it's clear that we trust each other implicitly."

Joyce did not miss a beat in confirming what Gwen had said.

"Mr Grundy, I have a successful career myself, a lovely home all paid for in Ireland, plus I will receive the very valuable stocks and shares left by my late father; it is right that Mum's home should go to her granddaughter and great-granddaughter, who have been living with her and keeping her company for the past four months. I'm happy to be the legal guardian and executor of Mum's will and I'm an equal match for my brother if he should launch a challenge, so Beth would not have to deal with that alone, if it should happen."

"Alright then, if you're sure. I will have the legal papers drawn up and contact you when they are ready to be signed." He stood up to indicate that the meeting was over and offered a very dry, wrinkled and mottled hand to shake theirs as they both left, privately thinking, as he had done so many times over the years, how sad it was that money and possessions caused so many rifts within families.

#

Joe was eating toast and jam at the kitchen table, watching his brother, Freddy, larrup peanut butter all over his. On top of that he placed several slices of banana and then, finally, chocolate spread, having used the same knife for all three toppings. Freddy was a living, breathing dustbin as far as Joe was concerned and he felt quite nauseous just watching the goo slip down Freddy's chin.

"Freddy, why the effing hell do you have to be so gross, I feel ill just watching you. Look at the bloody mess you've made of the peanut butter and chocolate spread jars, all mixed up now, you moron."

"Joe, leave him alone; it's Saturday morning and it's the one day where anything goes as far as breakfast is concerned, you know that. Just let him enjoy it in peace. You could do with eating a bit more yourself," his mum said, "how about some cereal or fruit?"

"No, I'll puke if I eat anything else now, after watching him - look, he's even got chocolate spread in his hair!" Martha began wiping Freddy's hair with a damp cloth, but she was focussed on Joe as she did it. She always knew when Joe had stuff he needed to say, the criticisms of someone else were always a giveaway, ever since he was little.

"What is it Joe, have you got something on your mind?" It was a few moments before he spoke, whilst he watched her cleaning up Freddy and was obviously mulling over whether or not this was the right time to ask a big question. He decided it was.

"Yes, but nothing bad, nothing to worry about. I was just wondering Mum – it's Easter in two weeks and I thought maybe Beth could come and stay for a bit. She and Holly could have my room, I'll bunk in with Freddy or on the sofa," he said, knowing without asking that there was no way he'd be allowed to share with Beth. "Her aunty Joyce wants Gwen to have a holiday with her in Ireland, at her flat, but there isn't room for Beth and Holly too and Gwen won't leave her on her own with the baby. Beth hasn't been home for almost five months now and I keep going up there, to stay with them, but it would be good for Beth to have a change too, don't you think?"

37

"Well Joe, I'm sure I have no objections to the idea, but is there a chance Beth's parents will be angry if she doesn't stay with them? Won't they expect her to stay there, with them?"

"No Mum, they've said she can come home any time, as long as she's alone – no baby. How could Beth do that, eh? They're mad, or cruel, or something. Perhaps Beth could go and see them whilst she's here and we could look after Holly for a couple of hours, I don't know. It's just an idea, I haven't said anything to her yet."

"Well, it's an idea, for sure; your dad's going to be away on the lorry the whole of Easter, so it won't interfere with one of his weekends home, but I'll check that he has no objections first." Martha was thoughtful for a moment, but decided she needed to be straight with Joe. "Actually Joe, there may be changes at Beth's parents that she's not aware of. You know that the Pro-life group I belong to meets outside the hospital and abortion clinics on abortion days, don't you? Well, some of us met last Saturday, intending to have a silent prayer vigil outside the S.K.I.L.L. Clinic, to pray for the tiny lives to be aborted that day and their poor parents too, but there was no-one there – it had a 'for sale' sign outside and looked completely shut down. Has Beth said anything?"

"No, she hasn't, but I don't think she has any contact with them normally. They haven't moved away, have they?"

"No, I don't think so, because one of my friends said that Ray Gregson was in a bit of a scuffle in a restaurant last week – she'd been there with her husband and witnessed it all. He was quite drunk apparently, but I don't know why and we shouldn't draw wrong conclusions. Anyway, leave this with me and I'll call your dad this evening, see what he thinks about Beth coming to stay. Now, both you boys, let's have your rooms tidied before you go off to football this afternoon; off you go, I've got peanut butter and chocolate spread to sort out now, haven't I Freddy!"

Molly was in a foul temper, as usual. She'd been furious with Ray since February, when she'd found out that he'd been deceiving her about the clinic, having told her it was closed for refurbishments when it was actually closed following a medical negligence tribunal. Ray had been found guilty and the sale of the clinic was now his only means of paying the vast costs of the case. What on earth he would do for an income in future was a question he could not answer, however many times Molly nagged him about it.

Home was dismal right now and there was no clinic to escape to, so most of Ray's afternoons were spent in one pub or another, bleating to anyone who would listen about how unfair life was sometimes, how badly he had been treated by the General Medical Council. Whisky had become his liquid lunch of choice, which bolstered him sufficiently to get home in time for dinner.

"Can you believe it Ray, our selfish madam of a daughter is paying us a *visit* during her week-long stay with the Lehman's – THE LEHMANS, I tell you. She'd rather stay in a paltry terraced house, crammed in with that dimwit Joe and his mother and brother, than stay in the comfort of our house in her old room. I'm speechless, I really am! You'd think Martha Lehman would have told her she should stay with us, wouldn't you? Speechless, I'm speechless."

"You don't sound speechless, if only that were true," Ray mumbled to himself as his head vibrated with her every syllable. He hung his jacket up in the hall and wandered unwillingly into the kitchen, wondering if his dinner would remain in his stomach without it reappearing. In contrast to Molly, his own speech was as slow and lifeless as his movements, as he pulled out a chair and sat gloomily at the dining table. "Why is she coming at all, when she's made little or no contact since we went to Dad's funeral in February? Is she bringing the brat with her?"

"I hope not. I'm not ready to be a grandmother, I'm not *old* enough to be a grandmother and I don't want the neighbours … people, to think I am. How can she be so thoughtless, especially when we're still sending her money each month?"

"Well, that will have to stop, because we can't afford to keep sending her money – we're virtually bankrupt Molly."

"Bankrupt? You didn't tell me things were that bad Ray, we can't be bankrupt, we just can't. Beth's still sixteen, still school age, so don't we have to keep supporting her, legally I mean?"

"I think so, yes, but if we file for bankruptcy, we may be exempt. Look Molly, I just can't worry about this now, not with everything that's going on with the clinic, it'll just have to wait. Why don't you phone up the school, they'll know. Now, what's for dinner?"

#

On the Wednesday before the Easter weekend, Joyce drove Beth and Holly to the Lincoln Transport Hub and saw them safely on to a coach bound for Bristol. Joe was getting a coach up to Bristol to meet them and travel with them back to his home for a week's break. It would be a squash at Joe's house, but he was getting used to sleeping on sofas, with all the trips to Lincoln in the previous five months and was happy to give Beth and Holly his room.

The following day, Joyce and Gwen drove to East Midlands Airport to catch a flight to Dublin. Gwen had finally agreed to a week away, once she knew she wouldn't be leaving Beth alone with Holly.

The airport departure lounge was bright and busy, like most airports, with massive windows overlooking the runway. Whilst Joyce went off in search of two coffees, Gwen sat on a rigid blue chair in a long row of the same and watched the planes come and go. Despite numerous flights during her life, she was always excited at the thought of flying and in awe at the weight of planes lifting off the ground so easily. As she sat there with her own thoughts, she suddenly became aware of Joyce holding her arm and shaking her.

"Mum, Mum, can you hear me? Mum, look at me, answer me." Gwen slowly turned to see the worried expression on her daughter's face and smiled. "Are you alright Mum?"

"Of course I'm alright, what do you mean? Have you got the coffees?"

"Yes, I have, but I've been trying to get your attention for a minute or two. Where were you, because you weren't here with me?"

"I don't know what you mean Joyce, I've just been waiting here for you and watching the planes. Now, let's have that coffee before it goes cold."

"No Mum, you were not responding to me, as if you didn't hear me. Are you sure you feel ok?"

"Stop worrying Joyce, I'm fine, now sit and relax for a while until our flight is called. Did you get any sandwiches?"

"No, you didn't ask for sandwiches, but I've got some biscuits in my bag. Hold my drink and I'll get them out," but Gwen just turned and continued looking out of the window and Joyce, watching her for a few moments, made a mental note to get her mum checked out once they got to Dublin.

#

Martha had forgotten how much she enjoyed holding babies, since Freddy was now ten years old. Holly was guzzling away contentedly at her bottle whilst Martha rocked them both gently under the canopy of the swinging chair. Joe and Freddy were kicking a ball backwards and forwards to each other at the far end of the garden, though Joe was a little preoccupied, wondering how Beth's visit to

41

her parents was going. They didn't expect her back for a couple of hours, unless things went terribly wrong at the Gregson's house; Beth had told her mum and dad that she was on her way and, although she was anxious about the visit, she had refused to let Joe go with her, insisting that she needed to go alone.

Molly opened the door before Beth had got half-way up the long garden path. The massive tubs either side of the front door were just as she remembered them, always crowded with pansies, juncus and alyssum, whilst trailing fuchsias overflowed luxuriously in dazzling pinks and purples from the hanging baskets above. As Beth reached the front door there was an awkwardness about the two women, neither of them knowing whether they should hug, kiss or shake hands, having grown even more remote from each other over the past five months. In the end they just shared a half smile and a nod.

"Don't stand there entertaining the neighbours Beth, come in. Your father's in the kitchen making a drink for us all." She held the door wide for Beth and, surprisingly, rested a hand on Beth's arm as she walked past.

"Hello Dad, how are you?" Ray turned from the fridge with a jug of milk in his hand and smiled, but made no attempt to come towards her.

"I'm fine Beth, come and sit down and I'll pour the tea." Molly put a plate of biscuits on the table and the three of them sat down together, not quite knowing what to say. "Are you on your own, or did you bring the little one?"

"Holly Dad, she's called Holly. No, I left her with …….. I thought I'd come on my own…..… I didn't think you'd want me to bring her."

"Quite, well, you're here now. I take it Mum and Joyce are in Ireland and you're staying with the Lehmans, but we thought you should have stayed here, with us."

"You won't accept Holly Dad, so how could I?"

"You know why Beth, because you've thrown away your future when I could have sorted that problem for you.

42

As things are, your mother and I are continuing to pay for your stupid decision, but it's done now, it can't be undone, so let's move on."

"I know, but you'd be paying anyway, if I were still living here, because I'm still school age. Don't worry, as soon as I'm old enough that will change."

"The point is Beth, we are no longer in a financial position to keep sending you money. My business has …….. is …….. over, I'm having to sell the clinic. We may have to sell the house too, I don't know yet."

"What do you mean? I don't understand."

"We're facing bankruptcy Beth. You don't need to know the details, just, it's over." Ray's voice was hard and cold.

"Well, I'm glad in one way, at least that means no more babies die in your clinic. I'm not glad that you and Mum may lose your home though, so what will you do?"

Molly had been quiet long enough and leapt into the conversation sharply.

"I've been in contact with your old school; you have to register with some sort of continued education in Lincoln if you won't come home, otherwise your father and I will be in trouble for breaking the law for that too. I have the forms to give you here, on the table, so don't leave without them." Immediately, Molly knew she'd said too much by the fury written on Ray's face.

"How exactly have you broken the law already?" Beth was scared now; would her father end up in prison? She was shocked to realise she still cared so much. Blood really must be thicker than water.

"Never mind, your mother said too much. Fact is, the money stops now, because you have enough left in your allowance from us over the last few years to cope, until we know more. Now, is there anything from your room upstairs that you want, if you're not coming home to live again? We may let your room, to professional people, for business stop-overs or something, like we did for Finn Orlandson, though he never paid."

Beth was shocked by the finality of her father's words – that she would never again live with her parents – that they would never accept her with a child in tow.

"OK, I'll go and have a look, if that's what you want." Ten minutes later she reappeared in the kitchen with a backpack stuffed full of underwear, t-shirts and pullovers, plus her old teddy which she'd give to Holly. She then picked up the school forms from the table, folded them and slid them into the front pocket of the backpack. "That's it, you can give the rest to charity or whatever, I have all I need now." She turned as she went towards the front door. "Do you want to meet Holly ……. now …… ever? I'm here until the weekend, let me know," then she left and heard the door close swiftly behind her. She knew that the chances were slim to zero, that she'd hear from her parents again before she returned to Lincoln and the now familiar wave of sadness swept into her as she retraced her steps towards the bus stop.

#

Gwen had refused to see a doctor in Dublin, insisting that she was 'just tickety-boo' and that Joyce always worried too much about her. She was sure she'd be fine now that she was back home. She'd really enjoyed her week in Joyce's flat, looking around a few of the sights of Dublin, shopping in Arnott's and Dunnes for a few presents for Holly and Beth, but home was where she really wanted to be, near to

Walter. Joyce had not intended to return to Lincoln, but a few more 'absent moments' in Gwen's week away had convinced her that she needed to see her mum safely home again.

Within minutes of settling down on her own sofa, after travelling most of the day, Gwen soon fell asleep and began snoring gently, like a purring kitten. She barely stirred the whole evening and Joyce decided to just cover her with a blanket and leave her in peace, before she turned the lights off and headed to her old bed. She was looking forward to seeing Beth and Holly when they got back the next day and drifted off to sleep lost in that happy thought.

At 8.30am the following morning though, Joyce was surprised to find Gwen still sound asleep on the sofa, exactly where she'd been left the night before. Joyce opened the curtains and made no attempt to be particularly quiet as she tidied papers and straightened the cushions on the chairs, but still Gwen remained far away in the land of nod. This was unusual, almost unnatural, Joyce thought as she made them some toast and a boiled egg apiece and a cup of tea, then she went back to rouse Gwen.

"Mum, Mum, are you awake? I have some breakfast ready in the kitchen," she said as she removed Gwen's blanket and shook her shoulder gently.

"Oh dear, whatever time is it Walter? I was in a really deep dream just then."

"It's me Mum, Joyce, are you ready for a cuppa?"

"Yes, in a minute, but where is Walter? Is he still in bed?"

"No Mum, he's not, he's ……. do you remember we came home from Dublin yesterday, on the plane?" Gwen sat up stiffly, trying to leave her dream behind and return to now, but she struggled.

"I've got the most awful headache and sore neck Joyce, I must have slept awkwardly, I don't think I've been to bed, have I?"

"You haven't, no; you looked so comfy that I left you on the sofa. Come on, breakfast is getting cold in the kitchen." Joyce took hold of the two dry, ageing hands reaching up to her and pulled her mum upright, then helped her to the bathroom while the teas went cold in their mugs.

#

Beth was waiting at the coach station when Joyce arrived to collect her, with a very happy Holly wide awake and burbling in her buggy. The bright, beaming smile on Beth's face when she saw her aunt arrive lifted Joyce's mood immediately – she'd missed them both more than she'd anticipated – they'd become quite a close family unit over the past few months, she realised with happiness.

"Beth, it's so lovely to have you back home with us, I'll put your bags in the boot whilst you sort out Holly. How was your trip?"

"The journey today was fine, bright and sunny all the way from Bristol and the coach was half empty, thankfully, so I could spread out our stuff over two double seats. Travelling all day with a baby isn't easy, but Holly was so good and slept a lot of the time. How was Dublin and how is Gran?"

"Dublin was great, just what Mum needed, but I'm sure she'll tell you all about that over supper. You'll notice that she's become rather forgetful all of a sudden, but it's probably just the last few months catching up with her. She keeps forgetting that Dad has gone and it's upsetting her when she's realises the truth, but she'll adjust, hopefully. Now, let's get home, I want to hear all about your week with Joe and his family, plus your time with your parents."

Within minutes of being strapped into her car seat Holly started grizzling – it was that time of day.

"Can we put some music on Joyce, it calms her, especially if I sing along, for some reason?" Sure enough, the grizzling stopped almost magically as the two women sang along with Michael Bublé, both happy to be back in each other's company again.

#

Martha and Joe were busy putting a fresh duvet cover on his quilt and putting his room back to normal after Beth's visit, Joe still angry at her parent's attitude.

"The Gregson's are really shitty parents Mum. Beth is very upset that they didn't want to meet Holly, again, their own grandchild – she's nearly four months old for goodness sake – what is the matter with them?"

"Joe, we don't know what goes on in other people's lives, we mustn't judge. I've told you already that their clinic is up for sale, so something bad must have gone on somewhere, but you're right, I don't know how they can cast their only daughter adrift like that. May-be she should just have turned up with the baby, not left her with us, I don't know."

"No, they don't deserve her, or a grandchild, they just don't. I might go around to their house later and tell them what I think of them."

"You leave it Joe, you don't want to risk making things even worse for Beth; also, Ray Gregson is not a nice man and he might get physical and hit you or something, you never know, so stay away, promise me." Joe grabbed a pillow and stared at her for a long moment, contemplating her words.

"OK, I won't go, but someone should tell him what a shitty person he is and thump him, or something." He started stuffing the ancient, flattened pillow into a fresh pillowcase and bit hard down on his lip as he remembered the last time he'd seen Ray. "You're right Mum, I think he's capable of being violent, because he pushed me over hard when I had a go at him in Lincoln, he was so angry."

"What? Look, you need to step back a bit Joe, don't get in the middle of other people's problems, especially family problems – I'm sure Beth didn't ask you to, did she?"

"No, she didn't," then he threw the pillow on the bed and left the room.

#

The paramedics arrived within fifteen minutes of Joyce calling 999 and were quickly ushered into the small living room, where Gwen lay motionless on the sofa, but still breathing. Beth waited in the bedroom with Holly, out of their way.

"How long has she been like this? Can you tell us what happened leading up to her falling unconscious?" The larger of the two women was asking questions whilst they both examined Gwen.

"Yes, we flew home from a week in Dublin two days ago and she's been complaining about a headache ever since – she's been rather forgetful too, forgetting that my father died just after Christmas, asking where he is and so on. When she woke up this morning she started complaining of an intense pain at the back of her head, so I went to get her some water and paracetamol tablets and, when I got back two minutes later, she was unconscious. That was about twenty minutes ago, when I phoned for you. Do you know what's wrong with her?"

"No, not yet, not for sure, we just need some details from you, as much as you can remember."

"Well, that's all really. She's been increasingly forgetful and complaining of headaches, nothing else. Very sleepy, but we have been away for a week, so may-be she's more tired than I realised."

"OK, but just say if anything else comes to mind." Joyce watched as they went through a well-practiced routine:

A (alert, no), V (verbal ques, no response to being spoken to), P (pain, no response to a strong hand squeeze), U (unresponsive in any way). Airway (clear), breathing (noisy but steady), pulse (normal), circulation (pressure on fingernail, blood reappears immediately pressure removed), blood glucose level (finger prick machine, normal, no diabetic hypo), oxygen level and blood pressure normal. Finally, an OPA tube was inserted into Gwen's mouth, to stop her swallowing her own tongue, then an oxygen mask was put over her mouth and nose. The women worked rapidly and efficiently, all the while stating what they found aloud and committing it to memory, to be recorded as soon as possible.

"What do you think is wrong, can you give me any idea?" Joyce was increasingly anxious as all this testing failed to cause any reaction in her mum.

"We can't say for certain, her vitals are steady just now; my guess is that she's had a stroke, either a thromboembolic or haemorrhagic stroke, put simply a clot or a bleed on her brain, though how severe a stroke we can't say until she's been assessed at the hospital. We can't take her to your local hospital I'm afraid, she'll have to go to the specialist stroke unit at Lincoln County Hospital, but it's not too much further for you. We'll get a carry chair from the van and take her there now; if you want to come with us in the ambulance you can, but just you." Within fifteen minutes of arriving at the house, the paramedics were loading Gwen into the ambulance and Joyce climbed in too, one paramedic driving and the other alerting the hospital to their impending arrival whilst continuing to monitor Gwen, as they sped along through Lincoln.

Once again, Beth was alone in the house with Holly whilst one of her grandparents was desperately ill in hospital. As she switched off her mobile having brought Joe up to date, she had an overwhelming sense of déja vu.

#

The estate agent was none too complementary about the clinic building, as Ray showed him around. Ray suspected this was more to do with keeping the suggested market price low for a quick sale, rather than because there was anything wrong with the building itself, but he found himself being defensive and unwilling to accept the criticisms coming at him. He also needed top dollar when it was eventually sold.

"The building is very dated, it hasn't been modernised in any way and would sell more quickly if you'd installed new double glazing throughout. There's no way this could be marketed for anything other than a business concern; it's not really suitable for flat conversions, retail or private accommodation."

Ray bristled inside.

"It's a grade ıı listed building, with restrictions on whatever improvements we'd hoped to make when we bought it four years ago. Hell, we can't even change the front door without approval and selecting from a limited range, so changes have been made within those restrictions. We have a fully functioning clinical procedures room installed, state-of-the-art heating and hot water system, automatic internal doors, plus quality antique furniture in keeping with the building's style, so I would have thought this was tailor-made for any medical businesses. Is there any market demand for medical properties?"

"Um.... not a lot, I'm afraid. If you need a quick sale, as you've implied, you'll be selling at below the usual market value – probably between £300,000 and £400,000, but I can get back to you with a more accurate assessment when we've measured up and done a full recce."

Ray was angry and made no attempt to disguise the fact.

"No, it has to sell for more than that ....I know it's worth a lot more. I'll get other valuations and let you know if I want to proceed with you. I'm sure you can see yourself out." The agent left immediately, Ray slamming the door angrily behind him as he watched his visitor climb into his Mercedes and drive away.

Fifteen minutes later Ray walked despondently into his house, wondering just how long it would actually remain his home.

"Incredible, just incredible, the idiot wants to sell the clinic for less than half a million Molly, but we need £600,000 to meet this damned negligence pay-out and solicitor's fees."

"What about insurance Ray? You must have had some medical liability insurance or something, won't that cover it? I've asked you about it several times but you always avoid discussing it. What about Finn too? Isn't he responsible for any of this mess?"

Ray looked over at the drinks cabinet, craving his usual refuge in alcohol.

"There's no insurance Molly. I worked in private practice, not with the NHS; the Medical Defence Union demands thousands of pounds a year to insure anyone and we just didn't have it ...... I thought we'd be fine until we got going better, until we were in a healthier position financially, but I never .... I don't know what the answer is. Finn Orlandson has done a runner too, we won't get a penny out of him."

"You idiot, you absolute bloody idiot, what were you thinking?"

"I think we'll have to sell the house too Moll, so you'd better start looking for a smaller one somewhere. Is there any whisky left …… or a bottle of red …… or *anything* to drink?" Unusually for Molly, she didn't utter a word, just headed to the drinks cabinet seething silently.

#

Later that evening, having struggled to eat the spaghetti bolognaise Beth had cooked for them both, Joyce sat quietly with a glass of wine, sipping thoughtfully. Wondering exactly what she was going to tell Ray, whether she should even bother contacting him yet, she decided to get it over with and wandered into the hall and picked up the phone.

"I don't know Ray, it's no good asking me all these questions, we won't know any details until she's had a full assessment, an MRI scan, whatever. I'll call you tomorrow night again, when we hopefully will know more of what's going on."

"But have they said it's permanent? Is she going to die or, worse still, stay alive but brain dead? I won't have that Joyce, you know I won't. I don't want her being a vegetable, on a machine Joyce, it's not acceptable."

"Slow down Ray, stop jumping the gun. We don't know what's going on yet. I'm tired so I'm going now, I'll call you tomorrow night." She put the phone down and puzzled at her brother's sudden concern, when he'd shown none when their dad was dying five months earlier. Was some normal human concern for a parent finally creeping in, or did he have a hidden agenda? Joyce sensed she may just face a battle ahead.

#

MAY

Gwen had been in a coma for five weeks. Joyce and Beth had been taking turns in spending some time with her each day, holding her hands, talking to her, reading aloud from her favourite Mary Stewart story, Thornyhold, singing her favourite Vera Lynn songs, all in the hope that she would hear them and regain consciousness, but so far without any response. Each evening Ray would call for a very brief update, but made no offer to come and help with these activities, claiming he was too busy with the clinic. In truth, a buyer had been found for the clinic, but Ray had been forced to accept a low price because time was against him. His house was also now on the market and he and Molly had been busy looking at cheaper properties to buy, but he wasn't going to admit this to his sister, not now.

The doctor was standing at Gwen's bedside when Joyce arrived and she was hopeful of some good news from him, but none came.

"I'm afraid there's no improvement in your mother's condition, which is a worry. Uninduced comas rarely last more than four weeks and we're now well beyond that. The longer she remains in this state, the more chance there is of complications, infections, pneumonia and so on, so we need to continue to monitor her closely. She could still begin to show signs of response in some small way, but with each day that passes that becomes less likely. Sorry I can't offer you more than that." He was methodical, clinical and unemotional, just offering a weak smile before he wandered off to his next patient.

"Oh dear mum, where are you? Can you hear me? Are you ever coming back to us? What should I do?" Joyce stroked her mum's arm as she stared into the lifeless face, so pale and fragile against the stark white sheets. She was a pitiful site with tubes and wires everywhere, a tracheostomy at her throat, catheter lower down in the bed, feeding tube from her throat taped to her face, but Joyce knew all these treatments were Gwen's best chance of survival, however undignified they seemed. She settled herself down and opened Thornyhold, chapter nine, then began reading.

#

Beth grabbed the phone on the third ring, hoping it wouldn't wake Holly, who'd taken a long time to get settled, as was normal in the evenings. Her father's voice took her by surprise, as she hadn't spoken to him since Easter in April.

"Oh, hello Dad. No, Joyce is still at the hospital, but she should be home soon as it's nearly nine-o-clock and visiting ends at eight. Shall I ask her to call you back?"

"No, you can tell me, has there been any change since the weekend?"

"No, there's been no change, unless something happened today. I won't know until Joyce gets home. I sat with Gran for a couple of hours yesterday and read her book to her, but there were no signs that she heard me."

"Well, something will have to be done, she can't go on like this. It's degrading, there's no dignity being wired up to machines endlessly, so we'll have to make some decisions. Tell Joyce I'll be up next weekend; I'll come alone and I'll sleep in Mum's bed, I won't do a hotel this time. Please pass on that info Beth, I'll see you then. Bye." The line went dead, abruptly, without any enquiry about her or Holly. How many more times could her father hurt her, before she stopped caring? As she was pondering this, she heard Joyce's car pull into the drive, so she opened the door to welcome her home with a hug, which she herself needed as much as Joyce obviously did.

#

Martha was waiting in the doctor's surgery for her well-woman appointment, which was long overdue. She thought perhaps she was having an early menopause because she hadn't had a period for three months, but she was only forty-one so may-be she was worrying unnecessarily. As she sat looking through a well-thumbed magazine at least six months old, she became aware of two women near her talking in rather loud whispers, obviously deliberately ensuring that their juicy information would travel quicker than the spread of headlice in a classroom. Martha hated gossips tittle-tattling about people, but she was human after all and couldn't stop herself from tuning in to the information spewing out of their mouths, once she realised who they were talking about.

"You know, he's been struck off, lost his clinic, the lot, truly. My Doreen went there only a few months ago for a termination and all was fine then – it was her third, she always went to him. £300, sorted, no hassle."

"You're kidding, that big S.K.I.L.L. Clinic in town? Really? That's been there for years, so what went wrong do you think?"

"I don't think, I know, because my friend's daughter Sophie was the secretary there. You wouldn't believe what went on. They had some scheme going on there for students who were getting sponsored for taking part in stem cell research for something or other. That's where the name comes from: 'Seeking Knowledge Intent on Lengthening Lives,' or something like that. Anyway, these students would have terminations in return for sponsorship, not legal, so he got caught out when a student got seriously ill after an abortion. Sophie helped get him shut down apparently. He's had to sell the clinic and now his house is on the market too, probably bankrupt after being sued and paying for solicitors and all."

"Well, I'm really shocked. You wouldn't think that things like that went on, would you? Terrible, he deserves to get shut down then."

"I know, but not sure where Doreen will go next time – she's just terrible at using birth control. Have to use the NHS I suppose, but then it's on your records, isn't it?"

Just then Martha heard her name being called and had to leave her eavesdropping behind with her magazine, but she couldn't help wondering how all this would affect poor Beth, or if she even knew? She walked in to see the waiting doctor and tried to refocus on her menopause.

#

Beth had been talking to her gran for about fifteen minutes, holding her hand and telling her about the first messy attempt to start weaning Holly, when she noticed Gwen's eyes open and stare at her. The unblinking eyes showed no recognition, no emotion, just remained blank, but they were definitely open for the first time in nearly two months. Beth quickly pressed the buzzer for a nurse to come, but it was several minutes before anyone arrived, by which time the eyes had closed again.

"She opened her eyes and looked at me, honestly. I was just talking when I noticed, but then they shut again. Does that mean she's waking up ….slowly?"

"May-be, but let's not get too excited just yet. We'll get the doctor to come and see her – he'll be doing his rounds shortly."

"My aunt is outside walking the baby. I'll go out so that she can come in, she should be here when the doctor comes around." Beth left excitedly to find Joyce and tell her the news they'd both been waiting for. Fifteen minutes later, Joyce watched as the doctor gently examined her mother, hoping that he would confirm an expected waking from the coma.

"I'm afraid you shouldn't get your hopes up too high just yet. Coma patients frequently move into what is called a vegetative state, where they may open their eyes, moan, even cry sometimes, but that does not automatically mean they're on the road to recovery. About fifty per cent recover consciousness, the rest don't and a prolonged vegetative state will often result in infections, pneumonia and a need for acute hospital care, so ......we just wait and see. How long that lasts is anybody's guess. I'm sorry, I don't want to give you anything other than the truth, no false promises, but it doesn't hurt to stay hopeful." Joyce quietly absorbed everything the doctor had said, but she couldn't shift one horrible word from her thoughts ....vegetative. Ray would not like it, not one little bit.

#

"Mum, are you serious? He's been struck off, lost everything and the house is on the market? What will he do, how will they live? I'm sure Beth doesn't know any of this because she would definitely have told me. Should I tell her, do you think?" Joe was at the kitchen table studying when Martha got home and shared this information with him.

"No Joe, definitely not, we don't spread gossip. I'm only telling you *in case* it's all true and she phones you to offload – you won't be able to help or say anything comforting if you have no idea what's going on. Forewarned is forearmed, as they say. If it's all true she's going to be upset, despite how badly she's been treated by her parents – they are *still* her parents at the end of the day. We have to trust that her aunty Joyce is the adult in all this and she's probably got Power of Attorney over her mother's welfare, so stay out of it as much as you can Joe. Just be there for Beth, if she needs you. Now, back to your studies, I know you have deadlines to meet with your coursework, so head down and I'll make us all a sandwich - sorry I disturbed you." She watched as Joe tried to refocus on his studies, knowing it was a lost cause; she busied herself with bread and ham as she marvelled, not for the first time, at how much Beth and Joe had both been forced to grow up over the last twelve months.

#

Molly was about as far from 'happy' as it was possible to be. She and Ray had been unable to refuse the offer on their house, even though it was £35,000 below their asking price, because time was their enemy – they had to pay their legal dues by the end of July, which gave them roughly ten weeks to complete on the sale and move. The house they were contemplating renting for a while was pathetically small in Molly's opinion – how could she possibly entertain 'her ladies' in such a humble house, a bungalow for goodness sake, when she had been 'queen bee' for so many years. It just would not do; she'd rather move out of the area all together than lose face amongst her 'friends.'

"Ray I can't live here, I just can't. It's claustrophobic, plain, characterless, it simply won't do. We must surely be able to afford something better than this hovel?"

"Molly it's not a hovel; it's clean, it's in good decorative order, it's very small compared to our house I'll grant you, but maybe it will have to do until we can find something better ….afford something better. It hopefully won't be for long, if fate is on our side for once and I get my inheritance."

"Whatever do you mean Ray? Your mother seems to be hanging on to life, it could be years before she pops her clogs?"

"No, I really don't think it will be too long before she joins Dad. I'm going up to Lincoln at the weekend remember. I intend to discuss the possibility of withdrawing these treatments which are sustaining her at present. Quite apart from our needs, it's degrading seeing her dwindling away week by week, tubes coming out of or going into every orifice, catheter and urine visible, it's disgusting, she has no dignity left and it shouldn't be allowed to continue. There has to be something I can persuade the doctors to do quietly, unofficially, if I can get to them without Joyce hovering all the time."

"Ray, you know as well as I do that euthanasia is illegal in this country. Aren't we in enough trouble already without you breaking the law again? I should have thought you'd learned your lesson by now."

"You don't understand Molly; we'll have very little capital left once our legal dues are paid and I have no job to go to, nor do you. We need my inheritance if we're going to get out of this mess and back to where we belong in society. I've been my own boss for far too long to go back to slaving for someone else for a pittance. Come on, I'm getting depressed in this poky hole now too, let's go for a drink somewhere. You can drive, I need a whisky," then they slammed the door of the bungalow hard behind them, without a backward glance.

#

One week later, Ray arrived in Lincoln mid-afternoon and immediately dumped his bags in Gwen's bedroom. It would be a trial staying in the small house with his estranged daughter and her baby plus Joyce, but he had no choice – he simply didn't have money to spend on a hotel visit, especially when it might turn out to be longer than a couple of nights.

Joyce made them all a simple ham salad for dinner followed by a supermarket trifle for desert and, to her surprise, Ray produced a bottle of red wine to go with it. The bottle was soon empty, Joyce having enjoyed only one glass and Beth none.

Conversation was difficult, mostly about Joyce's business in Dublin and Beth's decision to register at Lincoln College to follow a two-year course in early years childcare. Ray decided not to broach the subject of exactly where Beth planned to live whilst studying, once Gwen had died; he realised that not only were they both in denial about the minimal chances of Gwen recovering, but also that there would be an horrendous argument if he discussed his plans to sell Gwen's house immediately he inherited it. No, best to stay shtum.

Beth had cleared away the dinner things and gone to have a shower before bed, whilst Joyce relaxed on the sofa and gave Holly her final bottle of the evening. Ray settled down opposite her with a glass and his own bottle – whisky.

"Wow, you're knocking back the old alcohol a bit tonight Ray, don't you think you should slow down?"

"Don't start Joyce, you're not my mother – you're not anyone's mother actually" and he snorted with laughter. His words stung and his dribbling laughter both annoyed and disgusted her - he was clearly getting drunk. The need to retaliate reared it's ugly head and she wondered, not for the first time, why they reverted to being horribly childish siblings whenever they were together.

"No, it just never happened for me. I don't know how you and Molly ended up with such a great daughter though - two negatives making a positive, or something!"

"Very good Joyce, very good, very droll," as he topped up his glass for the third time. He gazed properly at Holly for the first time that evening, more out of curiosity than any sense of caring. "That child doesn't look anything like Beth. Shame"………. more snorts of laughter.

"No, I've wondered about that. She doesn't look anything like Joe either and they're both very dark, but you'd think she'd resemble one of them, wouldn't you?" Joyce smoothed her hand over the baby-soft golden curls, as fine as gossamer. "Joe's a great lad, he'd make a fine dad if only they were older, but far too young right now."

"Why would she look like him? He's not the father Joyce," ……. more snorts of laughter.

"Really? I just assumed he was, but Beth's never discussed it, so I didn't ask. Do you know who the father is then?"

"Sorry, can't possibly say, she'd have a fit if she knew." This time he snorted so hard that whisky came shooting out of his nose, all over his jumper and he curled up in hysterics.

"You mean *you* know but *she* doesn't? How can that be possible? If she was conscious, she'd know surely?" As Joyce's words left her own mouth, she knew what Ray meant. "Oh no, she wasn't drug-raped, was she? Ray, get a grip of yourself; have you ever talked to her about this?"

"Nope, she's was in denial about the whole pregnancy and wouldn't talk about it until it was almost too late for an abortion. Anyway, enough now, it's all in the past."

"But if you *know* and she doesn't, it must be someone you *know of*, someone who's stayed at your home, someone from work …is it?"

"Clever, very clever, you'll go far my girl," then he poured himself a fourth whisky, slumped back in the chair and fell asleep almost instantly with the glass still hugged to his chest. As he sat there snoring, whisky dangerously close to spilling all over him, Joyce wondered if any sister had ever loathed a brother as much as she did right at that moment.

#

Joyce and Ray walked into the hospital ward together, only to be told that they'd have to wait whilst Gwen was washed and turned by the nurses, to avoid bed sores. Ray felt repulsion creep through him at the sight of numerous geriatrics, all at various stages of disease and deterioration, languishing in their beds. He felt almost physically sick and had to fight the urge to leave, but he knew he had to remain to get this business over his mother sorted. When they were finally allowed to visit Gwen she was still obviously comatose, which filled Ray with revulsion. Whilst he remained at a safe distance at the end of the bed, Joyce sat and took her hand and began speaking to her as if she were conscious.

"Hello, Mum, look who's come to visit you – it's Ray. He's driven all this way just to see you – do you think you could open your eyes for him?" She waited for some small sign or response, but nothing came.

"She can't hear you Joyce, she's brain dead, you're wasting your time." He remained standing, unwilling to either sit down or to touch his mother. "We should speak to a doctor and see what her prognosis is."

"We know what her prognosis is Ray, we've had it explained to us. She's in a vegetative state and has a 50% chance of recovering consciousness, so we need to keep talking to her – she may well be able to hear us you know."

"No, it's pathetic, she's virtually gone Joyce and you need to accept it. It's dreadful watching her deteriorate like this, day by day, week by week, all pride and dignity stripped from her. It's immoral, it shouldn't continue." Joyce gritted her teeth and tried to keep her voice down, but it was difficult.

"What do you mean … 'watch her ….day by day, week by week…' it's the first time you've been anywhere near her since Dad's funeral four months ago, so don't come the high and mighty with me now Ray. She opened her eyes for Beth last week, she's still in there somewhere, we just need to be patient."

"Don't you understand the word 'vegetative' Joyce? What version of our mother do you think will re-appear, if she does wake up? She's not going to bounce back to normal, she'll be a dribbling mess in an adult nappy – do you really want that for her? For us? I don't."

"You don't know that, no-one does. Why don't you just go, because this will be upsetting her if she can hear you. No, in fact, let's both go and get a coffee and discuss this Ray, because we both need to know exactly where we stand

and we don't need Mum or Beth to be listening." As they turned and walked out of the ward, neither of them noticed big fat tears trickle down Gwen's face and seep into her pristine pillowcase.

#

The hospital café was almost empty, that lull between the breakfast rush ending and the lunchtime rush beginning, so it was easy for Joyce and Ray to find a secluded table away from anyone else who might earwig on their conversation. They each sat with a strong coffee, Ray to clear the brain fog from too much whisky the night before and Joyce to make her livelier after a restless night; battling with thoughts about Beth's drug rape and who the culprit might be had tormented her all night, but the unbelievable aspect was that Ray actually knew who it was and yet did nothing about it, did not tell Beth and did not press child rape charges against the culprit at the time. Why not? What sort of hold did the perpetrator have over him that prevented him from putting his daughter's interests first? Her head began a dull throb in the background which, history told her, was a sign of worse to come.

"Right Ray, you obviously have set ideas about how the next stage will play out, so let's hear them."

"No, I don't, it's just that Mum cannot continue like this indefinitely, it's pathetic. It's unpleasant for us all Joyce; we need to sort something out, for her sake and ours, so that we can all get on with our lives. Quite apart from us, what do you think this is doing to Beth, spending her free time reading to a slowly deteriorating vegetable, when she should be at school?"

"Oh, so *now* you care about Beth, but last year you didn't, is that right? Don't use her as an argument to suit your own selfish agenda."

"What? What exactly do you mean by that?"

"Ah, you don't remember telling me about the biological father of Holly then? Was that too much whisky loosening your tongue?" Ray's face went ghastly pale as he struggled to remember exactly how much he'd said the previous night, whether he'd actually named his ex-partner, Finn Orlandson, as the father. "Hah, you can't recall what you said, can you? I can tell." Joyce grinned in triumph, hoping he'd let the name slip this time. As he frantically searched his memory, the temptation to dig further got the better of her, so she took a chance. "Your colleague? Lovely blonde curls like Holly? I bet Beth would pin-point him in a nano-second if I told her. Come on, name the bastard that abused your daughter right under your nose."

"Shut up Joyce. I know you won't upset Beth, you care too much about her. Now, get back to Mum's situation and what we should do about it. Personally, I think we should just remove all tubes and machines and just let her slip away, let nature take it's course."

"No, we're not giving up on her, not yet, not just because you can't hack it."

"I think you'll find that, as the older sibling, my opinion will carry weight."

"Mum gave me Power of Attorney after Dad died, so I don't think so Ray."

"Financial Power of Attorney maybe, but not medical Power of Attorney – I'm right, aren't I? I know, because it never occurred to her that she'd become this ill so soon, did it?" Joyce remained silent; he was right and she was not at all sure that her opinion was as valid as his, being younger. She stared into her coffee, miserably contemplating his words, as the pain in her head began to increase noticeably.

#

Beth had had a busy day with her School Age Mother (SAM) Project Worker, Lizzie and her Educational Welfare Officer, Briony, sorting out her plans for September. They had helped her register for her course at Lincoln College, as well as fill out the applications for the financial support she was eligible for. She had been shocked to find out that her parents were legally bankrupt, though she had no details of why, but the official letters were the evidence she needed to qualify for the financial support available to her. Lizzie had supported her since she moved to Lincoln the previous December and Briony since February; she now viewed them as friends, though she didn't ever see them socially.

Holly was sitting happily in her baby bouncer whilst Beth peeled potatoes for dinner, when they heard the front door open and close gently. Joyce didn't call out her usual greeting, she just stayed quietly sitting on the small stool in the hall holding her head, so Beth called to her instead, whilst she gathered the potato peelings and put them in the bin.

"Hi, I'm in the kitchen with Holly, we're getting supper ready. Do you want a cuppa?" It took a huge effort for Joyce to get up off the stool, but she managed it and went to find Beth and Holly.

"Yes, that would be great Beth, thanks. I need some painkillers for my splitting headache too, so could you please bring them to me? I need to lie down for twenty minutes, then I'll tell you about the hospital over supper." Beth smiled and nodded, then turned to flick the kettle on, understanding that Ray's visit was taking its toll on her aunt as much or more-so than Gwen's illness was.

#

Ray did not eat dinner with them in the kitchen, preferring a tray supper in front of the television whilst watching some money programme. This was something of a relief to both women, but for very different reasons.

"Basically, there's not a lot to say about the hospital today. No change in Mum, all her vitals are steady, but no improvement in any way. Let's hang on to the positives though – there's no sign of any infection, all her organs are functioning as they should, so let's just keep hoping and praying that she stays well. How was your day?" Joyce tried to avoid mentioning her conversation with Ray by changing the subject.

"I'll tell you about that in a minute, but you haven't mentioned Dad. How was he with Gran? Did you notice any reaction in her when he arrived?" Beth would not be diverted so easily, which Joyce expected, but she didn't want to upset Beth so needed to choose her words carefully.

"No, not a flicker of recognition I'm afraid. Much as I dislike my brother, he is her son and I thought his arrival might just stir some memory in her, but no. We had a bit of a disagreement about her long-term care, hence the headache, but we'll sort it out, don't worry. Now, tell me about your day."

"It was good, really good. The 16-19 Bursary Fund is a discretionary bursary award from individual colleges and it looks as though I qualify, so Lincoln College should give me financial support to buy books, help with travel expenses and so on; I should also get vouchers for my lunches. Also, the Care to Learn people should give me up to £160 per week to pay for childcare, which will be amazing, if I get it. I feel really positive about this course because it should lead to a career after two years, if I work hard. It won't be easy and I'll miss Holly during the days, but it's for both of us and I can do some of the work online, so it should be OK."

"That's great Beth, I'm so relieved for you. What exactly is the course and have you told your parents yet?"

"No, I haven't had the chance and they haven't really shown any interest, but I'll probably discuss it with Dad some time. It's a BTEC National Diploma in Childcare – the extra brilliant thing is that it's free, so hopefully I'll be able to manage without a student loan, but that's there as a last resort if I have to." She sat with a genuinely big smile on her face, which Joyce hadn't seen too often over the past six months. Not for the first time, she marvelled at what an amazingly strong young woman Beth was turning in to.

"Wonderful, I'm really pleased for you and you know I'll help out a bit if you need me to. Now, shall we celebrate with another cup of tea, because my poor head won't cope with wine tonight."

"Yes and thank you Joyce. You go and lie down again, I'll bring it to your room, you look shattered."

"I am, thanks love" and she wandered off wondering if Ray was once again nursing the whisky bottle in the other room.

#

As Ray's luck would have it, Joyce developed a full-blown migraine headache and spent the next two days resting in the subdued light of her bedroom; she ate very little, but Beth made sure she had a constant supply of fresh water beside her bed. With Joyce out of action, this gave Ray an opportunity to visit Gwen in hospital alone, where he waited for a chance to speak privately with a doctor.

He could not cope with more than ten minutes at a time with his mother, watching saliva trickle out of the corners of her mouth incessantly and staring at the bland face totally devoid of expression. This was not his mother, in his opinion, it was just a shell left behind once she'd left, so to speak. Consequently, he spent a large portion of his time in the hospital just wandering around in the vicinity of the ward, hoping to snatch some precious time with her doctor.

On the second day, he left briefly for a coffee and a sandwich at lunchtime and found the doctor at Gwen's bedside when he returned.

"Ah, doctor, I'm so pleased I've caught you." He extended his hand in greeting, which the doctor accepted, though this was unusual in hospital. "I'm Ray Gregson, Gwen's son. I wonder if I could have a little time with you, in private, to discuss my mother's condition?"

"You could, but right now I'm doing my rounds and I have another twelve patients to review, so you may have a considerable wait ahead of you. Is it really necessary, because I've given your sister all the information we have for now?"

"Yes, I know, but I'd like to discuss her long-term situation and I think, to date, you've only shared the short-term with Joyce."

"We don't know the long-term I'm afraid but, if you care to wait, I'll see you briefly after my rounds."

"Thank you, I'll wait." As the doctor wandered off to his next patient, Ray sat down and opened his newspaper, doing his best to avoid even looking at his mother as much as possible.

#

Joe wandered into the kitchen to find his mum folding washing on to the kitchen table. She was humming one of her favourite songs as she gazed up at him mid-fold.

"Well, you look like the cat that got the cream; what's put that big grin on your face then?" Martha was pleased to see Joe so happy for once; the pressure of coursework and deadlines was so intense that he'd looked permanently serious since his return from Lincoln the previous month.

"I feel happy, that's all. I've just got off the phone to Beth and she's been telling me about her plans, continuing her education and so on, it's all sorted. She's registered at Lincoln College, but I'll tell you all about it over dinner – I'm going to see a couple of mates right now, have a kick around in the park or something. By the way, she wants me to go up for a while when the school term ends, which is only a few weeks away for me, unless you have any real objections."

"No, not at all and I'm pleased for her. Having Joyce there has made such a big difference to her, but I thought you were planning on getting a job for the summer, weren't you? It's a chance to save a little, I thought."

"Yep, I know, I may even get one in Lincoln for the summer, for five or six weeks, if I can. It all depends on Gwen and how she is. If she's well and comes home, Joyce will go back to Ireland for a while but, if not, Gwen may be in a care home or something – we have to play it by ear. Beth's dad is there right now but he probably won't stay long, he and Joyce don't get on. Not sure why he's there because Beth says he obviously hates visiting the hospital and he seems to be in a permanently grumpy or difficult mood. Anyway, I'll be back before dinner, bye." Martha folded the last of the washing, wondering what had got Ray to Lincoln when his father's funeral was the only time he'd visited in years, especially when there was so much going on in his life at home right now. Was Gwen more seriously ill than Joe or Beth knew, was he genuinely worried about his mother at last, or was there an ulterior motive? She knew she'd have to wait to see how this one played out, but privately hoped Beth's new plans wouldn't be scuppered by her difficult father.

#

By the time the doctor came to find Ray he'd been sitting beside Gwen's bed for a further three and a half hours. He felt overwhelmingly impatient, with nothing to do but wait for so long, but he knew he had to stifle it in the doctor's presence.

"Ah, Mr Gregson, I'm afraid my rounds took longer than expected – now what is it you want to know?"

"Well first off, how long is my mother likely to remain in this vegetative state?"

"That really is a 'how long is a piece of string' question, I'm afraid. Your mother has been in this condition for seven weeks now; when we get past four weeks it's called a continuous vegetative state and this could go on for up to twelve months, when it changes to a permanent vegetative state diagnosis. Of course, she won't be able to remain in this hospital bed for a year, she'll have to be transferred to a hospital setting for chronic conditions or a long-term care unit. The bottom line is, the longer she remains vegetative, the less are her chances of regaining consciousness. At present she remains relatively healthy, she's breathing unaided, but the risks of infection, pneumonia etc are ever-present, so we have to be vigilant. She's in the best place at the moment Mr Gregson, she's being well cared for, so try not to worry too much at this stage. Is there anything else you'd like to ask?" Ray scratched his head, searching for the right words to express his thoughts.

"Look, is there anything you can do to …….. alleviate her suffering? This is dragging on, she could be in severe distress and all this is agonizing for her family, seeing her like this."

"Mr Gregson, as far as we can tell your mother is not suffering any acute pain. If I understand you correctly, what you're actually asking me to do is illegal in this country. We can't end lives simply because of the discomfort of the family having to deal with a sick relative."

"I don't see why not – you can in the USA. No, what I really mean is, I've heard that injections of morphine, or whatever, to relieve suffering, often help the patient to just slide away quietly, even if that's not the intention, am I right?"

"Your mother is not in pain, as I said, so why would I give her morphine? I'm afraid that is not an option. Now, is there anything else?"

"One last thing doctor; I would like my mother to pass with some dignity and, as she is now, there is no dignity. If you were to just discontinue using the apparatus which is sustaining her life, she'd surely just drift off in her own time, wouldn't she?"

"Your mother is not on a ventilator, she is breathing unaided and her heart is beating unaided – she's not on a life-support machine Mr Gregson. The tracheostomy at her throat is to clear any fluid build-up, so that she doesn't choke on her own saliva, but it *is* in place should she need a ventilator. Her waste is syphoned off via a catheter and weekly manual extrusion because she's not consciously controlling those functions, but otherwise she's independent, just vegetative. Withdrawing these critical care procedures is unthinkable at this time. Now, if there's nothing else, I really must go, goodnight." He left before Ray had a chance to speak again but, as he walked away, he was in no doubt as to the exact nature of Ray Gregson's wishes.

#

It was ten thirty that night before Joyce and Beth heard Ray come in through the front door. They had both gone to bed, but his loud, clumsy, drunken entrance had ensured they were both now wide awake. Holly was a sound sleeper and would normally only be woken by hunger later in the night, but not on this night. The deafening crash of him tripping over the buggy in the hallway, knocking over the small table and smashing the vase of flowers that usually sat beside the phone, followed by a burst of vile swearing, woke her too, so the whole disaster was eclipsed by a now screaming baby.

"What the hell are you doing Ray?" Joyce could smell the whisky immediately she came into the hall. "It's late, you've woken us all up and now there's a whole mess to clear up, you're disgusting. I think you should pack your bag and go home first thing tomorrow, this is just too much."

"Oh, bugger off, go back to bed and just leave me here on the floor, I'll stay here for a bit," then he curled up amongst the debris and closed his eyes. " 'Squite nice here acherly."

"Ray, get up. We're not leaving this mess here, we need to clear up the broken glass ….Ray!" Joyce went to the kitchen and filled a jug with cold water, then came back and poured it over his face and head.

"What the fuck are you doing, you stupid bitch, just piss off," then he scrambled to his feet and fell into the living room, where he collapsed on to the sofa. Joyce set about clearing up the mess on the floor, now made worse by an extra litre of water, suddenly realizing that not only had Holly stopped crying but also, amazingly, that her migraine had gone too. Sometimes you really do have to search for the silver lining, she thought to herself as she swept up the glass.

#

Ray was still snoring on the sofa when the other three Gregsons left for the hospital late the following morning. Beth went for a walk in the park with Holly and took a slow route to the hospital, having arranged to meet Joyce outside at lunchtime with a few sandwiches she'd pick up on the way. Joyce went straight to Gwen and was sitting reading to her sometime later when the doctor reappeared.

"Ah, Miss Gregson, I'm glad you're here; I've popped in before I go on duty to suggest that we have a meeting here at the hospital with you and Mr Gregson, with myself as Gwen's consultant physician, the ward sister and possibly the ward manager or a member of the Patient Liaison team, to discuss your mother's situation and future care. Having considered what your brother said last night, I think it's important to have a continued care plan in place for her, possibly transfer her into a long-term care setting, all these sorts of things so that you can see a way forward."

"I'm sorry, what do you mean, '*considering what your brother said*'?"

"Mmm, I wondered if that was a family opinion or just Mr Gregson's; I think you'd best discuss that with him, it's not my place to comment, but a meeting between the relevant parties should help to clarify things, so we'll sort out a time as soon as possible, OK?"

He was gone without further comment, but he'd left Joyce with an uneasy feeling in her gut. 'What's that so-and-so been saying, I wonder?' She closed the book, patted Gwen on the back of her hand and wandered off to find Beth, convinced that another unpleasant clash with Ray was almost inevitable and that the advice and presence of the care team might just keep it civil. Time would tell.

#

Ray surfaced from a deep and unpleasant dream at around lunchtime, with a disgusting taste in his mouth. His neck was stiff, his head throbbed and the daylight streaming through the living room windows made him wince. 'Where is everyone? Why is it so quiet? What time is it?' Basic questions he had no answer for. The sudden sound of the phone ringing felt like a bomb exploding inside his head, so he staggered to the hall to grab it and make it stop hurting him.

"Ray? Is that you? It's me, Molly."

"Yes, I know, I'll call you back in a bit."

"No, you won't, you'll speak to me now. You haven't called for two days, what's going on?"

"Molly, stop shouting, lower your voice ….. please."

"You're still drunk, aren't you! I can tell from your voice!" Anger seeped through every syllable and knocked against his brain like a woodpecker. "Ray, you need to your keep your wits about you, get this mess sorted and get home. I can't handle everything here on my own. The estate agent keeps bringing the people who are buying the house and it takes a lot of effort to keep it immaculate. I've looked at three more houses for us Ray, but they just aren't good enough, simply too small and in the wrong areas – what am I supposed to do Ray? You need to be here, to help me.

Now, sort yourself out and stay off the whisky, for both of our sakes. Call me back when you've had a strong cup of coffee!" She was gone, much to the relief of Ray's very sensitive eardrums.

Shaving in front of the bathroom mirror, he saw what had been so tender whilst in the shower a few minutes earlier – a large and unpleasant looking welt on his left cheekbone which was a dark shade of red-turning-purple and a deep cut on his chin.

"Bugger, I look as though I've been in a brawl," he said to a pair of grey-ringed and puffy eyes staring back at him but, try as he may, he couldn't remember how they got there.

#

Beth was once again sitting holding Gwen's hand, telling her about Holly's delight at her new Jumparoo and sitting independently surrounded by toys; it was a godsend, a gift from Joyce, freeing up Beth's arms for a while whenever she put Holly in it. She was mid-sentence when she suddenly realised Gwen was watching her, eyes wide open, staring unblinking at her.

"Gran, can you hear me? Gran? Blink if you can hear me," …… nothing. "Gran, can you squeeze my hand? It's me, Beth, your granddaughter," …..again nothing. Beth called for the nurse and continued asking Gwen to respond whilst she waited, but the eyes were shut again by the time the nurse arrived. "She opened her eyes again, she really did, but she didn't seem to recognise me," Beth said excitedly.

"Ok, that's great. I'll note it on her chart; that's the third time that we know of, but it may have happened more when she was alone. It might mean something, but you never can tell with brain trauma, so let's not jump the gun here; we'll talk to the doctor, when he's doing his rounds."

Beth couldn't help it, despite the nurse's warning and her excitement a while later when she told Joyce was bubbling out of her.

"Truly Joyce, she stared at me for a few minutes - this may mean she's waking up, don't you think?"

"It might mean that Beth, it's encouraging, but it's not the first time and we haven't seen any progress really. Let's stay positive though and hope for the best, shall we? *Positive things happen to positive people* remember, that's one of Mum's favourite sayings, so fingers crossed. Now, let's go and get a cuppa and a slice of cake somewhere and I'll tell you about the meeting set up by the hospital." They walked away lost in their own separate thoughts, Joyce wondering what her brother was up to and Beth grinning from ear to ear at the thought of Gwen's possible recovery.

#

Ray sat at one end of the long table in the Patient Liaison Centre at the hospital, ready to take control of this meeting, or so he thought. His time in Lincoln was limited because Molly needed him back home, so dilly-dallying by anyone was not an option; he needed to get straight answers to straight questions or, more importantly, get *these people* to see common sense from his perspective. It was costing the NHS a ridiculous amount of money day by day, week by week, to keep Gwen alive unnaturally, or so he saw it, when she was clearly not long for this world in any case. Without all the medical interventions she would have died already, so why prolong the agony? Now, how to persuade them all diplomatically, without making enemies immediately, was going to be the tricky part. Persuading Joyce was going to be the monumental stumbling block, he knew that much before the meeting even got off the ground.

The room was bright and airy, windows wide open on this warm spring day, but that did nothing to lighten the intensity of the conversation which dominated the atmosphere. A jug of water and glasses were passed around whilst Gwen's consultant physician, Mr Osborne, plus his registrar, secretary and the advanced practice nurse settled themselves into seats opposite Joyce. A member of the Patient Liaison (PALS) team was the last to enter the room and sat at the opposite end of the table to Ray, in his direct line of vision.

"Right, I'd like to begin by ….." was Ray's attempt to control the meeting from the off, but he was immediately stopped in his tracks by the PALS officer.

"Excuse me for interrupting Mr Gregson, but I think it would be helpful if we began by introducing ourselves and to understand that the meeting is being recorded digitally, as well as minutes being taken by Mr Osborne's secretary. If we could begin with me, John Hanson of the PALS team and go clockwise, thank you."

"Rachel Dyson, advanced practice nurse."

"Philip Osborne, Mrs Gregson's consultant physician."

"Angela Lane, Mr Osborne's secretary."

"Harry Grant, Mr Osborne's registrar."

"Joyce Gregson, Gwen's daughter."

"Ray Gregson, Gwen's son!" His tone was already a tad impatient at being overruled immediately and he knew he needed to either regain control of this meeting without delay, or accept playing second fiddle to these people who seemed intent on prolonging an already-doomed life, as he saw it. "As I see it, my mother has shown no progress in all the weeks she's been lying horizontal in this hospital. She remains vegetative and, if it weren't for all the contraptions and machines keeping her alive, nature would have taken its course and she would have passed away gracefully, with dignity, a long time ago. Out of respect for her, I think that it's our duty to remove all treatments and let her slip away in her own time, saving unnecessary emotional pressure on her family and unnecessary financial pressure on an already cash-strapped NHS. It's logical, it's sensible, it's humane and it's the correct thing to do. So, unless there are any arguments to the contrary, I suggest this meeting can be a formality and we all take a vote on this decision." He looked around the table at what could only be described as six stunned expressions, each an exact mirror image of the others.

"Objection," Joyce almost bellowed "and don't over-rule me Ray!"

"Look, I have done my research on this and I know that it is legal to remove a feeding tube from a vegetative patient if medical opinion is that it is in the patient's best interests. What can my mother's quality of life be like, trapped inside a non-responsive body and brain?"

Rachel Dyson spoke up for the first time since introducing herself.

"Mr Gregson, that was the Liverpool Care Plan which you may be thinking of, which is illegal. From a medical perspective, there is a huge gulf between what you, as a healthy adult, perceive it to be like to be locked into a vegetative state like your mother's and what she is actually experiencing. Withdrawing her feeding tube assumes that your mother's life is not worth living, but we do not have the right to make that value judgement without clinical evidence that she is suffering. We believe that about 50% of patients in this condition are aware of what is happening and about 20% regain consciousness eventually; if your mother is aware and we were to withdraw her nutrition and hydration tubes, she would effectively starve to death and may well be aware of that unimaginable process and suffer horrendously." Rachel looked to Philip Osborne to reaffirm what she had said but, before he had a chance to speak, Ray beat him to it.

"No, I know that the British Medical Association and other top medical bodies are at the forefront of pushing forward the decriminalisation of abortion and assisted suicide – they want the government to agree to this so that euthanasia and assisted suicide are freely available in this country, as they are in numerous others."

Philip Osborne knew he had to set Ray straight.

"Mr Gregson, the entire medical profession still fundamentally works on the ethos of the Hippocratic Oath, which basically is to promote and restore harmony in the life of the sick. We do not wish to return to a pre-Hippocratic Oath, where medicine can mask as health care but can in fact cause death. If the law changes at some future point and it becomes legal for medics to promote and advise euthanasia, simply because of convenience or cost, where would the trust and faith in our doctors and health system be? Nowhere, people would become ever more fearful of coming into hospital and, furthermore, trust in our family members would deteriorate." The intensity of both Philip Osborne's facial expression and tone were not lost on anyone – this was not the first time he'd faced these challenges.

Ray was not yet ready to admit defeat though.

"I'm sorry, this is so wrong. We put sick animals out of their misery without question, so why not people too? Is it fair that my mother continues to suffer because we are behind many forward-thinking countries around the world? Isn't it time the opinions of the patient's family members were considered?"

Philip Osborne knew his own personal and professional opinions were in tune though and pressed further.

"Mr Gregson, such a scenario would weaken society's value of human life, it would damage trust in the medical profession, it would discourage the search for treatments for terminal illnesses, it would weaken investment in proper palliative care and, ultimately, patients would feel the pressure from their families to be euthanised when they really didn't want to take that route, just because they were perceived as a problem to be solved. No, this is not the way forward, even though I know you believe it would be preferable."

"But … I …"

"Right, I'm going to stop you right there," Philip Osborne stated politely yet firmly, if slightly louder than he'd intended; "we are all here to discuss the best options for your mother Mr Gregson, not to make a snap decision. Also, this is not a court of law Ms Gregson, so your opinion will be heard just as fairly as your brother's. Now, I think we should focus on your mother's clinical condition, because this will be the deciding factor in her future care, above all and any other opinions."

He stopped, took a long swallow of the water in front of him and gathered his thoughts for a moment before continuing.

"Now, before we make any decisions, we must first look at the condition Mrs Gregson is in at this time. We are confident that the evidence from successive CT scans and an MRI scan gives us a clear picture of what is actually going on. Although we have ascertained that she has suffered a stroke in the location of her brain stem, she is not what is termed 'brain dead.' She remains unconscious and does not respond to outside stimulation at present, yet her heart and breathing continue without medical intervention, so the level of brain damage is only partial and may not be irreparable. This situation could change at any time, of course."

Another break for a second swallow of water and a few moments to consult his notes, then he continued, pleased that Ray Gregson had not seized the opportunity to interrupt and resume his bullying tactics.

"She is receiving CANH, which is clinically assisted nutrition and hydration, which is vital to maintain life. She has a tracheostomy tube and she is catheterised, but there has been no sign of any infection caused by this situation, even though it is longstanding, so that is good news. Rachel, do you want to add anything?"

"Yes, thank you Dr Osborne. Mrs Gregson is not suffering from any bed sores, thanks to the nursing staff so, all in all, physically she is in a good condition for someone who has been comatose for so long. Although she has opened her eyes on several recorded occasions, this may have happened more often than we are aware, yet she shows no recognition of anyone during these times.

I believe we can be confident that she is in no overwhelming physical or emotional distress, or this would be obvious during these wakeful periods. I think that's all I need to add, thank you."

Philip Osborne decided it was an opportune moment to round things up.

"Thank you Rachel. So, in conclusion, it's my professional opinion that care should continue as it is currently, until we see signs of improvement or deterioration, at which time we'll reconsider the situation. My medical staff concur with this opinion, isn't that right Rachel and Harry?" Two heads nodded in confirmation.

Ray could see this meeting was not going as he wanted it to; he was like a dog with a bone and was not ready to give up.

"No, that's not acceptable. Without CANH, as you call it, my mother would have died peacefully, in her sleep at home probably, with some of her family around her. As it is, she'll no doubt die in a harsh hospital ward, all alone. Is that really what you want Joyce? We need to maintain her dignity, let her go now, not watch her deteriorate slowly over the next months just because you selfishly don't want to lose her. I'm here now, I can't stay indefinitely, she needs to go whilst we're all here together Joyce, you must agree surely?"

"No Ray, I don't. She's our mother and if there's any chance she can recover from this and enjoy watching her great-grandchild grow up for a few years, then she deserves to be given that time. She was happy before the stroke, before we went to Ireland, so why not give her more time to come back to us?"

"Because she's not going to Joyce, can't you see that? She'd be better off with Dad, wherever he is; she'd want to be with him, not prostrate in a hospital bed month after month. It's cruel and I won't allow it to continue. I need this sorted whilst I'm still in Lincoln."

"Why Ray? What's the rush? I can work online from Lincoln, I don't need to hurry back to Ireland, so you can go home and return when you're needed, not that you ever did before!"

"What's that supposed to mean Joyce? You're just being selfish, you're ...."

"OK, I need to redirect us back to the needs of your mother and what is best for her," Philip Osborne interrupted. "Now, prior to her stroke, did Mrs Gregson express any opinions on what should happen in the event of any illness which she may suffer? Did she write down or legally record any DNR/DNAR/DNACPR, or more simply, 'do not resuscitate' wishes? Did she have any religious beliefs which may affect the treatments she receives? Did she express any wishes *not* to have treatments to prolong her life? You see, it is *her* wishes which are important to consider, as we decide on a way forward."

"'No' to all of those questions, none that I recall and nothing legally recorded," Joyce stated.

"Did your mother give you or Mr Gregson Legal Power of Attorney concerning health and wellbeing?"

"No, only financial POA," Joyce said sadly. Why, oh why, had they not included health and welfare when they renewed Gwen's will, then she would be legally safe from Ray's intentions.

"OK," Philip Osborne continued, "I propose that we move Mrs Gregson to a palliative care ward within the hospital and monitor her condition carefully over the next weeks, possibly months. If her condition changes noticeably, then we will meet again to consider the options open to us. Palliative care can continue for up to a year, but I'm confident the situation will have resolved itself one way or another well within that time," then he sat back and looked around at the faces staring back at him.

"Right, if we're all agreed I'll get that written up and we'll arrange Mrs Gregson's move. Thank you everyone for coming."

"This is ridiculous, we're not done here, you'll be hearing from my solicitor," Ray said as he left the room without further discussion. Joyce watched him leave, wondering again why exactly he was in such a hurry to wave their mother peacefully off to the afterlife, when he hadn't cared two beans about her for quite a few years up to now. Money, it must be money she realised, but he was in for a nasty shock when that particular can of worms was opened.

#

JUNE

Molly and Ray had been in an Airbnb for three weeks, overlooking the beach at Weston-Super-Mare. As Molly leaned out of the open bedroom window she felt restricted and claustrophobic, despite the huge expanse of sand in front of her; the tide was out and she could not see the sea, which was at least half a mile away in the distance, but she still felt hemmed in.

"We can't stay here Ray, it just won't do. I don't know anyone, there's nowhere to go, nothing to do, no sense of a normal life at all."

Ray looked up from his laptop, momentarily diverted from the 'situations vacant' in the medical recruitment website he was poring over.

"That was the whole point of coming here Moll, away from people we knew witnessing our change of fortunes. It will have to do for now, until we can see a way forward."

"There's no light at the end of the tunnel though Ray. You have absolutely no idea of how to change our situation, of how to increase our income and of how to get us back where we were, where we belong, in the higher income bracket of society."

"Look, there's nothing I can do about all this immediately. There isn't enough money left to buy us anything bigger than a rabbit hutch, until my mother passes on and I inherit some funds; together with what we do have, that might be enough to get a suitable property back in our own neck of the woods, then you can resume your previous social life. You just have to be patient. In the meantime, I'm looking for half-respectable jobs where I'll have a position of authority or respect – I can't settle for less Molly, not after being my own boss and running my own clinic for so long. Look at this one here, not too far away:"

Health
Public Health

You will be required to work flexibly
working hours: 37 hours per week
Your role:

Devonshire Council is seeking to appoint an experienced and influential Assistant Director - Population Health & Wellbeing (Deputy Director of Public Health) to join our senior management team.

This is a strategic corporate role, working across the organisation and with partners to challenge, influence and transform services and to provide excellent public health services for Devonshire residents, achieving our aspirations and priorities for the future.

You will take a leading role in the development, implementation and delivery of national, regional and local policies, whilst providing expert public health advice and leadership to the Council, the Borough CCG, the Integrated Commissioning Committee and Healthier County Partnership.

About you:

With an in-depth understanding of local government, population, health and wellbeing and the health and care system, you will have a proven track record of delivering successful change management programmes along with the ability to design, develop and implement strategies and policies.

You will have proven leadership skills and operational intelligence with a commitment to citizen-led public health. Your ability to engage, facilitate and support local people and organisations to realise their full potential in improving the borough's health and wellbeing will be essential to this role.

You will have the ability to maintain effective, courageous and responsible public health advocacy and hold evidence of an up-to-date programme of CPD in accordance with the Faculty of Public Health requirements or another recognised body.

"Yes, I think this is right up my street Molly, I shall write an application today, now, so why don't you go for a walk along the promenade and then bring us some fish and chips in for supper, with a bottle of red wine – I have a really good feeling about this one."

\#

JULY

Joe was thrilled that school was over with for six weeks and wasted no time in catching a coach to Lincoln, to spend the holidays with Beth, Joyce and Holly. It was the first time he'd been away from home for the whole summer, but his parents were taking Freddy and a school friend to Disney Florida for three weeks and, at almost seventeen, Joe felt much more enthusiastic about a holiday job, his first taste of independence and time with Beth. He'd managed to find a position working in a Tudor-style café near Lincoln Castle, serving, waiting on table and washing up and he loved the freedom and earning his own money. Joyce did not ask him to pay any rent, because his presence allowed her to travel between Lincoln and Dublin for her work without worrying about leaving Beth alone. He was also really good at visiting Gwen on his days off and chatting away to her about the different characters he encountered in the café, very amusing if you were also by the bed listening. Joe also brought home a variety of café foods which hadn't sold during the day, which more than compensated for a few pounds rent in Joyce's opinion.

Beth set herself up as a dog walker for a number of neighbours who couldn't do the task themselves, for whatever reason. She could manage this easily with Holly in the buggy, just one dog at a time and she became a familiar face in the local parks, throwing a ball or a stick for one dog or another. This also gave her a little extra cash in hand too, which she was careful to save apart from a weekly contribution towards household costs, the same as Joe. The days and weeks bundled along happily and the evenings were relaxed, friendly times spent cooking, playing games, watching TV or taking turns to spend time with Gwen, who remained disappointingly comatose. It was quite a surprise then, or rather a shock, when Beth opened the front door to Ray one Friday evening.

"Dad, what are you doing here, why didn't you tell us you were coming?"

"Well, are you going to ask me in or keep me here on the doorstep Beth?"

"No, of course, come in. The others are in the living room."

"The others? Not just Joyce then? Is Mum home and you didn't tell me?"

"No dad, she's still in hospital, I meant Joyce and Joe …. and Holly."

"Oh, what's he doing here?"

"Just come in, we'll explain in a minute." Beth followed her father into the sitting room where three sets of eyes looked in his direction, surprise rather than pleasure written on their faces. "We were just having a cuppa Dad, would you like me to pour you one?"

"Yes, I'm quite thirsty after that drive up here, that would be good. Where shall I sit?" Joe immediately leapt to his feet.

"Here, sit here Mr Gregson, I can sit on a cushion on the floor." Joyce's eyes never strayed from her brother as he crossed the room and sat in the only armchair, knowing that hell would freeze over before he offered any thanks to Joe.

"So, why have you come and why didn't you let us know you were coming?" There was a definite tone of annoyance in her words, which made him glare at her.

"Well, it's *my* home too Joyce and it's also *my* mother who is wasting away in hospital, so I thought I'd come and see how she was getting on. Has there been any change?"

"Yes, some, but not significant. She's opening her eyes more often, but it doesn't last long and there's still no recognition of any of us, plus she hasn't spoken."

"Well, we need to have another meeting like we had in May. Her condition must have changed to some extent, one way or another, so it needs to be reassessed. If she's opening her eyes more but not communicating, it must indicate that her brain hasn't improved at all, that it's not going to."

"I could argue with you Ray but I'm not going to. We'll wait and see what the doctors think, but you really should have phoned and arranged a meeting before coming, because we may have to wait days or even weeks." Joyce was determined to remain calm in front of Beth and Joe, but she was rattled that her brother had turned up out of the blue and may be staying more than a few days. "Why have you come now Ray, without warning?"

"No reason, it was just a convenient time work wise, that's all." At the mention of work, as she handed him his tea, Beth thought it would be a good time to ask a few questions.

"So, how's work going Dad? Last time we spoke you said you'd had to close the clinic altogether."

"The clinic's gone Beth, I told you that. Nothing definite yet, but I have a few irons in the fire."

"What does that mean? I don't understand."

"It means I'm looking at beginning again, new openings, new businesses, new investment, but it's all still in the planning stages."

"Please tell me you're not opening another abortion clinic Dad."

"No, not that. A new direction, but I'm not ready to discuss it yet. So, why are you here Joe?"

"I'm here for the school break Mr Gregson; I have a job and I'm staying for six weeks, so that I can spend time with Beth and her gran – with Joyce and Holly too, of course."

"I hope you're paying rent then, contributing or something. Can't have you sponging of us."

Joyce was immediately infuriated at his attitude, especially as his own behaviour in the last year had been so despicable.

"That was totally unnecessary Ray and none of your business actually. You don't live here and you have no authority over anyone. Joe is contributing in ways you wouldn't even understand. Please don't spoil the evening by being unpleasant."

With the wind knocked out of his sails, he tried to think of another way to minimise Joe's presence.

"Where is everyone sleeping then, because I'll need a bed for a few nights?" Looking directly at Joe now – "I assume you're *not* sleeping in Beth's room?"

Joe was shocked by this, understanding the implications, but he knew he was a guest and didn't want to cause upset, so resisted the urge to rise to the challenge.

"No, of course not, I…." but Joyce cut him off mid-sentence.

"Sorry Joe, but I'm not having this. Ray, if you're trying to cause an argument and make everyone uncomfortable, then you're heading in the right direction, so just stop now or leave. I'm currently in Mum's room, Beth's in your old room with Holly, as before and Joe's in my old box room, on a single. So, if you're staying, you're on the sofa, that's all there is. If not, then there are plenty of hotels in town, your choice."

"No Joyce, it's alright, Mr Gregson can have the bedroom, I'll go on the sofa," Joe chipped in. "I have my sleeping bag in the wardrobe and I got used to the sofa at Christmas, when Gwen was still at home. I'll go and sort the room now," then he quietly got up off the floor and left, with Beth close behind him.

"Right, that's sorted then. I'll go out to the car and get my bags." As he left, Joyce marvelled first at how much more mature Joe was than Ray, despite his youth, as well as wondering how she was going to keep the peace over the days ahead.

#

In the subdued, dim light of her hospital bay at the end of the small ward, lying motionless in her bed at four in the morning, Gwen opened her eyes. She was too hot,

89

uncomfortable, unable to speak, locked-in, but no-one was there to notice her distress in the quiet of the early morning. How long did she remain like this? No-one will ever know, but it was an hour later that a nurse hurriedly called for the doctor on night duty.

At the same time, three miles away, Beth woke up and sensed immediately that something was wrong. She quietly checked Holly, still sound asleep, then listened outside her bedroom door for any signs of movement in the house, but nothing. Which must mean it was Gwen, but how did she know that? She was puzzled and suddenly afraid, fearing the worst, but she did not have the courage to wake up Joyce, only to face the ominous scenario from the hospital, or alternatively to unnecessarily disturb Joyce's sleep. Instead, she lay awake for the rest of the night, head on her pillow, watching the dawn slowly arrive through the gap in the curtains, dreading the day to come.

#

The rapid deterioration in Gwen's condition meant that Ray was able to persuade Philip Osborne to set up an emergency second meeting for forty-eight hours later, consisting of the same people as before. Ray was unhappy at having to wait even that short time, but the doctor wanted to give the new medication a time to begin taking effect, before he had to make decisions. The strong antibiotics would hopefully, at least, start to ease the pneumonia and begin to relieve the kidney infection by then, both of which had come on suddenly and acutely.

As they sat around the same table in the same room in the same seats, there was somehow a greater sense of urgency, for Ray if not for anyone else. To that end, he decided to take the lead on the conversation and hoped, this time, to maintain control.

"Right, the last time we were here, over two months ago, you assured me Dr Osborne that my mother was perfectly healthy, albeit comatose and in no obvious distress. This is obviously no longer the case, yet this was the very reason you were happy to continue her treatments and thereby prolong her life. From where I'm sitting, things are deteriorating rapidly and it would be a kindness to let nature take it's course and not extend her suffering." He glared at the faces all focussed on him and waited for a response.

"Mr Gregson, as your mother's consultant physician, I can state that the current complications, unpleasant though they may be, are not entirely unexpected. It is not unusual for comatose, bed-bound patients to develop infections and, hopefully, a course of strong antibiotics will do the trick. It's impossible to gauge conclusively whether there is any high level of distress, but the nursing staff have witnessed no moaning or groaning, no mumbling or crying, which would indicate pain or discomfort." Philip Osborne noted the nods of agreement amongst his staff.

Ray would not give up easily though and felt he was on more solid ground than in the earlier meeting, with the vast deterioration in his mother's condition.

"You stated before that my mother's heart and breathing were continuing unaided, but that level of independence has now gone. Without antibiotics, the infections would undoubtedly accelerate and she would end up drowning in her own secretions – why not just let that happen and allow her to slide away from this life uninterrupted. I'm not asking you to kill her, just let nature decide for her."

"Mr Gregson, as I have mentioned before, our main objective is to preserve life. Your mother is only in her seventies, no serious previous illnesses on record, no cancer or heart disease threatening her life at this time and, with the correct treatment, there is still hope that she will regain consciousness and go on to enjoy a happy and healthy old age. I do not agree with you that the kindest option would be to end her life and, if she is remotely conscious of what is going on, the distress of 'drowning in her own secretions' as you put it, unable to communicate fear or distress, would be horrific."

Ray was now getting impatient and frustrated – he'd thought he had a better chance of persuading these medics to agree with him this time, considering Gwen's current poor condition.

"You know Mr Osborne .... I'm sure you must know, that in 2005 the "right-to-die" lobby in the United Kingdom succeeded in passing the Mental Capacity Act in England and Wales, allowing .... no, sometimes compelling doctors to deny food, fluids and reasonable medical treatment to patients who are neither terminally-ill nor in the immediate dying process or in their last days; this included pro-euthanasia principles and was approved in subsequent court cases, so why is my mother excluded from this right?"

"You're right Mr Gregson – you've clearly done your homework – but since that initial ruling, the lobby has failed to make any gains in this country, like those seen in other countries."

"Look, euthanasia or assisted suicide is legal in Victoria in Australia, the Netherlands, Germany, Switzerland, some states in the USA, Belgium, Canada, Luxembourg, Colombia, probably more countries, so why are we so reticent here? It's madness. I know that you, as my mother's doctor, are legally allowed to withdraw treatment if she's in a continued vegetative state and certain not to recover – it's called passive euthanasia and you won't be prosecuted for it, so why not?"

"Firstly, many of those countries have not passed laws *allowing* euthanasia or assisted suicide, they have simply failed to pass laws to *prohibit* the practices. Secondly, we can't be sure your mother is beyond recovery, it's impossible to say at this time, so I'm not prepared to make that call."

He paused for a few moments, gathering his thoughts, before continuing.

"You know, once the taking of human life is made lawful, as it was following the British Abortion Act in 1967, it becomes acceptable and, eventually, it's regarded as normal. In my opinion, this end-of-life promotion is a medical horror which is spreading across the globe at an alarming rate.

In 2019 in the Netherlands, a doctor administered a lethal injection into an Alzheimer's patient whilst her relatives forcibly held her down – what part of that is acceptable Mr Gregson? I'm pleased to say that the doctor was charged with murder, but where are we headed if this becomes the norm and replaces the expectation to preserve life? Where will the trust in medics be? I'll tell you, it won't exist.

This insanity, this disease, this downward spiral towards euthanasia that is racing across the globe will mean that, once doctors are allowed to kill their patients, vulnerable patients like your mother will find that the right to die has become a duty to die. No, Mr Gregson, you will not get the answer from me that you want, no."

John Hanson of the PALS team could see how angry and agitated Philip Osborne was becoming and decided to intervene, redirecting the discussion back towards Gwen's immediate care.

"Can I suggest that Mr Osborne advises on the current situation and the way forward over the next week? Philip?" A clearly rattled Philip Osborne composed his thoughts before speaking.

"Now, I suggest we allow Mrs Gregson the opportunity to respond more positively to the antibiotics being administered; after all, although we expect the medication to have some effect within forty-eight hours, it is not usual to actually see that progress immediately – it may take a few more days. If she shows no sign of improvement by the end of a week, then signs of deterioration would most likely be evident and she would need more invasive treatment. We watch and wait, simply that."

Joyce had been watching Ray closely, trying to ascertain why he was again in such a rush to end Gwen's life. He had never been a loving son, rarely paid his parents any attention beyond birthday and Christmas gifts organised by his secretary yet, strangely, he'd been to Lincoln more in the last six months than in the previous six years. Why? Money, plain and simple, it must be. He wanted his inheritance and he wanted it now. His lost business, sold house and hoped-for new career must be the result of some catastrophe along the way, so more digging was required on her part. Maybe Joe's mother had told him about it, she'd ask him later.

"OK then, thank you everyone for your contributions, meeting over. We will, of course, inform family members immediately if there is any change in Mrs Gregson's prognosis." Philip Osborne stood to indicate that it was time to leave the room and watched as, once again, Ray Gregson stormed angrily away without further comment.

#

As Joyce later sat trying to erase Ray's words from her mind and focus on reading to Gwen, Joe appeared in the little hospital bay with two cups of coffee and a box of left-over almond croissants from the café. A sweet treat was just what Joyce needed after the meeting earlier and she marvelled at what a positive presence Joe was in their lives just now.

"Joe you're a gem, you really are. Yummy, perfect to tide us over until dinner time. How was your day?" Flakes of croissant fluttered down all over her pullover as she took a bite greedily, which made him laugh.

"Good, very good thanks, they're a friendly bunch at the café. Got some generous tips today too so how would you like some fish and chips from the chippy tonight? My treat?"

"Brilliant, perfect, couldn't be bothered to cook if you paid me. I'll text Beth so she doesn't start preparing anything."

"OK, do you want to go now? I can stay for a bit?"

"No. Let's finish our coffee here then we'll go together, have an earlier night, spend more time with Beth. I want to ask you a few things on the way home – not here." Joe was puzzled, but he didn't have to wait long and, twenty minutes later, they were meandering along in Joyce's car.

"I was wondering if your mum had shared any information with you about Ray and Molly Gregson … I mean the sort of information you may not have shared with Beth."

"Why, what's this about Joyce?"

"Well Joe, I'm going to confide in you, but I don't want Beth distressed unnecessarily, OK? At the hospital meeting earlier today, like last time, my lovely brother seemed to be in a tearing hurry to end our mother's life – I don't mean kill her, but he certainly wants it over with as soon as possible. He's shown absolutely no interest in either of his parents for years, but suddenly he's overly concerned, so money has to be at the root of it, but I can't think why. Can you shed any light on this at all?"

"Oh, I see. Mum did tell me something she'd heard at the doctor's surgery last month, but she doesn't like gossip and she just warned me in case Beth was upset – Beth hasn't said anything, so nor have I. All Mum said was that both the clinic and their family home was being sold because Ray had broken the law and was found guilty of a medical negligence charge or something; he had to sell up to pay the legal fines and compensation to a student – he had some legally dodgy business going on and got caught out basically."

"You don't know any details though? Is he bankrupt?"

"I don't know any more, sorry, just what Mum overheard, but I know it's something to do with the abortions at the clinic." Joe tried to wrack his brains for more details but couldn't remember any. "I know that Beth was really upset when she found out he ran an abortion clinic – she thought the clinic was something to do with research, but that was an add-on I think."

"Right, so it's definitely money then and he must think he's going to inherit a substantial amount, but he's in for a nasty shock in that case. Thanks Joe, I'll have to sort this out somehow." Joyce pondered this news for a moment, then decided to seize the moment to ask something else she'd been worried about. "Whilst we're sharing confidences, has Beth ever spoken to you about who Holly's father is? Sorry, but I automatically thought it was you until Ray put me right; don't get me wrong Joe, you're a great friend to Beth and an incredible support to us all, but too young to be a dad right now. One day, someone will be very lucky to have you as a dad," then she smiled and patted his knee for reassurance.

"No, she hasn't. I'm sure she doesn't know who it is and it's pissed me off big time not knowing; but I mean, how can she *not* know who it is? She was in total denial for so long that I think she must have just blocked it from her mind – I'm not sure she even wants to know. Puzzling that Ray knows if Beth doesn't, how can that be? He's not capable of ……. of doing that to his own daughter, is he? I think I'd want to kill him if he did!"

"Oh, good grief, no. As you know, there's little or no love between Ray and me, but he's not capable of incest, I'm sure. No, it's someone from work, someone who's stayed at their house – he all but admitted it to me last time he was here."

"Well, the only person who's stayed at their house, as far as I know, is a man called Finn Orlandson who was working with Ray on some project last year - Beth couldn't stand him, he gave her the creeps and she used to come over to mine whenever she could if he was staying."

"What did he look like?"

"Can't help there, sorry, I never met him. Do you think it was him? Why would Ray allow that to happen, to his own daughter, in his own house? What a bastard. Hang on though, Beth said she'd never had sex, so how could that happen?"

"Rohipnol, or some other similar widely known date-rape drug, especially effective when taken with alchohol – it sedates and causes amnesia – it's the obvious answer."

"Oh my God, poor Beth – we learned all about it at school in Year 11 – I bet she's never even considered that and she'd be horrified if she knew that bastard had abused her. How does Ray know? Why the hell didn't he get the police involved, charge the bastard with abuse of a minor, get him locked up?"

"He knows because it happened in their house, when this guy was staying – Ray couldn't deny it. He must have had some hold over Ray, something to do with the clinic." Joe was quiet for a moment, then another thought occurred to him.

"Beth loves Holly, I don't want that to change by her knowing who the father is."

"You say nothing, ignorance is bliss on this occasion. Just let her enjoy her baby, but you know Joe, the maternal instinct is known to be one of the strongest emotions possible and that baby is 50% Beth, so nothing will break that. If she does find out, we'll help her come to terms with it somehow. Now, we're home, let's go in and enjoy a nice supper, hopefully without Ray."

#

After six hours in a selection of bars in the town centre, Ray headed 'home' and once again all but fell into the little house in Lincoln shortly before eleven-o-clock that night. This time he managed to avoid knocking over furniture and smashing vases on his way to the living room, but he was clumsy enough to draw Joyce out of her bedroom when he plonked himself on to the sofa on top of Joe, who'd been asleep there for twenty minutes.

"Oh, for fuck's sake, what are you doing in here?" he growled at Joe.

"Ouch, you've winded me, get off. I sleep here, remember? Ever since you arrived and claimed the bed. GET OFF!" Joe gave him a shove and he landed on the floor beside the sofa. Just then Joyce walked in and witnessed the two men glaring at each other.

"Ray, this has to stop. You need to pack a bag and go, tomorrow, I've had enough. Joe, are you ok?"

"Oh, shut up Joyce. You can't order me out, you stupid bitch, it's my home as much as yours." He scrambled up into the single chair and watched her fussing over Joe, who was clutching his ribs uncomfortably. "Look at you, you're pathetic, fawning over a boy young enough to be your son. Why are you still here anyway? You're not needed here, just fuck off back to your mad mother and your pokey house, why don't you?"

Joe was shocked by this abuse.

"I …… I'm here for Beth, for Joyce …… I ……. you're a disgusting excuse for a father, do you know that? You're not worth the ground my father walks on, you're …"

"Enough, enough," Joyce shouted; she was angry and feared where this confrontation would end up, if she didn't nip it in the bud straight away. "Ray, I'm going to get some strong coffee, you need it, we're going to sort this out now, once and for all. Joe, you can stay or you can go and sleep in my room for now, it's up to you."

None of them had noticed Beth standing in the doorway.

"No, he can come and sleep with Holly and me, just for tonight and no, Dad, …… nothing will happen, before you ask. Dad I …. I don't know who you are any more," then Beth turned and walked sadly back to her room with Joe close behind her.

#

With two strong cups of coffee inside him Ray's head became a little clearer, but not much. Joyce was wired after her own two cups, determined to get to the truth, however ugly that might be.

"What's going on Ray? You've all but ignored us all for years, now you're like a fly on a bloody doughnut – we can't get rid of you. Come on, spill the truth, I know most of it anyway. I know you've lost your house, the clinic, you've broken the law in some way and had to pay compensation to someone as well as legal fees. What's going on really? Are you bankrupt, is that it? Are you wanting Mum to die so that you get an inheritance to bail you out?"

"How astute of you – got your little moles have you? Joe been filling you in on the gossip from his pain-in-the-arse mother, has he? Look, Mum's knocking on death's door as it is, it'll be a good thing for us all if she just sods off out of it and we all move on. Just imagine Joyce, you'll never have to set eyes on me or Molly again, won't that be bliss?"

"It certainly will, you heartless bastard. This is your mother, have you no compassion, no conscience? She gave you your life and you just want to take hers away from her. How could you?"

"Oh, just grow up Joyce, face reality. She's gone, she's not coming back, *we'd* be better off if she was dead and so would she. No-one lives forever and her time is clearly up, so just deal with it."

"What exactly do you think you're going to get Ray? I have legal Power of Attorney over her finances, remember? I went to the solicitor with her to re-do her will and you get nothing – not a brass farthing. Just Dad's medals, as before." Ray blanched, clearly shocked to the core. "Hah! That's taken the wind out of your sails, hasn't it?"

He got up and crossed the small space between them and stood over her menacingly, glaring down, as his words spluttered out of him.

"What and you get it all? That can't be legal, I'll challenge it."

Joyce stood up to face him, equal in height so not intimidated at all.

"Nope, not me – Beth. The house goes to Beth, I'm just the legal guardian until she's eighteen. So, you see Ray, all this hanging around has been for nothing, NOTHING."

"I don't believe you. I'm facing total ruin, TOTAL RUIN and you're telling me I won't get anything, not even a half share of Mum's estate? That can't be right. Beth's my daughter, not yours and she still remains my responsibility until she's eighteen. I'll challenge this Joyce, you see if I don't."

"Go ahead Ray, try and see where it gets you. Mum's will is a legally binding document, signed when she was fully compos mentis in front of old man Grundy and he's an absolute stickler for the rules. So, you'll be wasting more time and money if you try."

"But why does Beth get the house? She's just a kid. What will Molly and I do now? We've got next to nothing, no job, no income, just what's left of our house sale. This is a disaster, a fucking disaster."

"Perhaps you should have thought about all this before you broke the law Ray. You've been the master of your own downfall. What sort of a man are you? You flout the law, you put your own needs before other's always, even your own daughter. You stand by whilst she's sexually abused and do nothing about it. You virtually disown her whilst heavily pregnant and kick her out, whilst you swan off on a holiday, then you bleat about 'poor old you.' Who cares Ray, I know I don't. You get what you deserve – nothing."

Ray shoved her hard and she fell back down on to the sofa.

The raised voices meant that Joe and Beth now stood listening from the other side of the living room door. Ray pushed past them and stamped furiously out of the house, slamming the front door hard and almost shaking it off it's hinges. The two of them hurried into the living room to find Joyce sitting on the sofa, bent forward with head in hands, shaking violently, but they couldn't tell whether she was laughing or crying.

\#

The night was dark, raining heavily, as Ray pulled out of the driveway in his car and accelerated furiously away. His head was fuzzy, he could not make sense of all that Joyce had said, all he could see ahead was blackness and white flashes as he charged along at a terrifying speed. Ten minutes later he was racing along the A46 towards Skellingthorpe and the rain was getting heavier, the windscreen wipers having little or no effect, but his anger was forcing him on into blind rage.

The police car siren and flashing lights behind him added to his fury and he needed to lose them, so he put his foot down hard, almost doubling the permitted speed restrictions. The next moments were over in a flash – a flash of pure bloody devastation. His steering locked, he braked, skidded and careered across the carriageway, straight into the path of an articulated lorry coming in the opposite direction. Their combined speed increased the impact dramatically, crushing the driver's side of Ray's car and forcing it along sideways for five hundred metres, until both vehicles screeched to a messy halt, narrowly avoiding numerous other drivers out in the perilous conditions.

\#

Molly, Beth and Joyce sat silently at the hospital bedside in the intensive care unit, listening to the incessant beeping of the life-support machine. This was made all the more distressing as it was difficult to recognise Ray, so damaged was his head and face, swaddled in dressings. Molly repeatedly began crying loudly, then managed to regain control, only to lose it again a few minutes later. The doctor was speaking, but his words were not penetrating anyone's thoughts – just stunned shock ruled the moment. Joyce made herself snap out of the guilt that was plaguing her and tried to focus on what he was saying.

"At present, the severe head and facial injuries are making testing for brainstem reflexes difficult. The CT scan and the angiography have shown that there's acute hypoxic-ischaemic brain injury, which means that chances of recovery are slim to none."

"What exactly does that mean doctor, in layman's terms?"

"Simply put, it means that there is little or no blood supply to the cerebral centres, so no brain activity can be detected. There is complete and irreversible loss of brain-stem function – we don't anticipate any improvement with this, so you need to consider the immediate decisions which must be made. I'm sorry I can't offer you more hope."

"So, if all brain functions have stopped, it's only the life-support machines keeping him breathing and keeping his heart beating, is that what you're saying?"

"Yes, I'm afraid so. It's only mechanical intervention that's maintaining organ function. With brain death – we prefer the phrase 'total brain failure' nowadays – it's primarily the cardio-pulmonary criteria that governs whether or not life should be continued mechanically; the brain death diagnosis is a secondary one. Your brother's heart and lungs cannot work independently any longer, plus there is extensive trauma to his liver, kidneys, spine, fractured skull, most of his skeleton." At this point, Molly started sobbing inconsolably.

"Okay doctor, if we could have a while to make that decision, thank you." Joyce turned to the other two and took a deep breath before speaking. "Right, I suggest we go and get a drink in the café, because we've all had a terrible shock and we need to take stock, try to stay calm and talk about what has to be done." She stood and, between them, Beth and Joyce each took one of Molly's arms and led her out of the ICU ward.

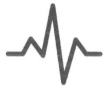

#

Joe was already waiting at the station with Holly when Martha stepped off the coach. After a brief but firm hug, Martha took the buggy whilst Joe picked up her small case and headed for the taxi rank.

"Where's Freddy Mum?"

"Don't worry about him, he's staying for the weekend with his best pal; he's still jet-lagged from our three weeks in Florida, so he'll probably sleep for most of the next few days anyway. Now, tell me all that's happened and how Beth is coping, poor lass." Joe gave her all the details in the taxi on the way to Gwen's house, settled her in with a cuppa and a sandwich, then left Holly in her capable hands whilst he caught a bus to the hospital.

#

At the farthest end of the hospital, cocooned in her own private world, totally unaware of the trauma being played out by her family not so far away, Gwen continued to lie perpetually motionless. Her infections had cleared, thanks to the powerful anti-biotics and the excellent care she was receiving from the nursing staff, so her life was no longer in any imminent danger and the status quo had been resumed.

Joe was beside her reading through the penultimate chapter of Thornyhold, having briefly seen Beth on his way in earlier. She knew he was nearby if she needed him, but her duty was with both of her parents at that time and not with her grandmother, who was stable for now; past difficulties can be put to one side when life and death decisions have to be made. Joe was so engrossed in trying to concentrate on the words that he was not aware that he was being watched, silently, by a mute listener with a gentle smile on her face. She remained watching, listening, smiling for ten minutes or so, before closing her eyes once more and enjoying the tale.

#

"No, I can't bear it, he can't be gone. He has to come back to me. How will I manage without him?" Molly was still distraught, but the sedatives were beginning to calm her a little and Joyce needed her to remain lucid enough to share in the decision making – she was his wife after all.

"Listen Molly, the doctors have done all they can but he's beyond further help. The only thing we can do now is to let him go, here, peacefully, whilst we're all with him." The doctor and nurse stood by, listening to this exchange, witnessing this sad truth, as they had done numerous times before.

"Why? Why can't they help him, bring him back? He's young, only forty-six. That old woman has been lingering for months, unwilling to let go of life, she's still being treated, yet they won't help her son."

"Their situations are different Molly, you must see that surely?"

"No, no I don't. They're just playing God, deciding who lives and who dies, it's not right. What's the difference, you tell me, I don't understand." She sobbed loudly, then sank despondently into a chair.

"Mrs Gregson, the difference is medically enormous. Your mother-in-law, whilst in a semi-vegetative state, is maintaining her life independently – that is, her heart and lungs are working unaided. Sadly, your husband is not so fortunate and would have passed already, were it not for the mechanical intervention keeping him alive. His injuries are extensive, beyond repair and he has, as I said earlier, total brain failure. Two doctors have verified, separately, that your husband is, to all intents and purposes, already dead, I'm so sorry." He turned and directed his next words to Joyce and Beth. "Now, can you tell me if your brother, father, had any religious beliefs – would you like us to send for a priest? Also, did he ever express any opinions about not extending life support beyond the accepted medical diagnosis?"

"No, thank you, he was not remotely religious, so no priest, pastor, whatever. He did have strong opinions about assisted suicide, euthanasia and that whole argument – he was in favour. Our mother has been semi-vegetative for some months, as you know and Ray was overly keen to remove any medical intervention sustaining her life. No, I'm sure this is the decision he would want us to make, thank you. Molly, do you want to add anything?" Molly was silent, just shook her head.

"OK, well, this is neither assisted suicide nor euthanasia – the extensive trauma to his body and brain has removed that argument. You can stay with him whilst we remove all the interventions, then share his last moments together, just let us know when you're ready. We'll leave you to talk for a few minutes." Joyce reached out and took Beth's hand and squeezed it tight in reassurance. Beth turned to Molly and tentatively, gently, stretched out her arm and took her mother's hand too.

Three weeks later, after a funeral that was a carbon copy of Walter's only months earlier, the minuscule gathering of five adults plus baby Holly left the crematorium. Molly decided not to return to the family home for the cake, tea and agonising conversations with her estranged family, preferring to get a taxi straight back to the railway station and home to her own mother in Tavistock. Following her mother's advice, she'd been accepted back into her previous life at a hair and beauty salon in town and would have to earn her own wage for the first time in twenty years, following an initial spot of retraining. '*No point in delaying, time to move on,*' was her new mantra.

Beth and Joe had gone for a long walk around the park, trying to get their heads around yet another big change in Beth's life. Beth was deep in thought, completely preoccupied and oblivious to the beautifully blooming flowers and trees all around them. The sun was dazzling, almost blindingly bright as it played hide and seek behind the taller trees, so they were glad of their sunglasses.

"You know Joe, it's strange, but I don't feel anything, nothing. Why is that? I know he wasn't a particularly good father, but he was *my* father nevertheless, my flesh and blood, but I feel nothing. Is there something wrong with me?"

"No, there isn't. I remember Joyce saying the same thing when your grandfather died and she was close to him. She said it's nature's way of helping you cope; you sort of shut down emotionally for a while, especially if you've had other traumas to deal with too, which you have, with Holly's birth, Walter's death and Gwen in hospital – it's been one hell of a year for you Beth, hasn't it?"

"Yes, I hadn't thought of it like that. I was scared for a while that I was more like him than I wanted to be, so I hope you're right."

"You're nothing like him Beth, you're not like either of your parents, thank goodness. I wouldn't feel the way I do about you, if you were like them." Joe wondered instantly if he'd said too much about his feelings, Beth had been through so much, but it was too late. She stopped walking and looked him straight in the eyes.

"What do you mean Joe, '*the way you feel about me*?'"

"Um, just that we've both grown up so much in the last year and .... I don't know about your feelings, but mine are changing somehow .... I feel protective towards you, I like being with you more and more, I don't know...... I like holding your hand and I'd like to do more, but I ......, I know I can't." Beth was puzzled, not sure of her own feelings, all emotions had been so jumbled up for her for so long. She opened her mouth to speak, then shut it again, before taking a big breath:

"Joe, you are my best friend, I trust you more than anyone and I love being with you too, but I don't know my own mind lately and ...... and, I can't risk making any more mistakes that might spoil our friendship. I'm not ready for anything else Joe, anything more, can you understand that?"

"Yes, I understand, of course and I won't push you, but can I call you 'my girlfriend' at least?"

"Um ...... yes, as long as there's no pressure, OK?" He smiled and gave her a quick hug, then started them both walking again.

"OK. Now, why don't we go home via the hospital and pop in on Gwen, see how she is? Focus on the living, not the dead."

"Good idea, when exactly did you get to be so wise?" She gave him a gentle shove and took his hand, then they headed for the park gates and the bus stop.

#

Martha and Joyce were enjoying a glass of wine each and a bowl of mixed nuts at the kitchen table, with Holly asleep on Martha's lap. The two women had got on well since they'd met a few weeks earlier following Ray's crash and Joyce was grateful that Martha had returned to be supportive through the funeral. Joyce could recognise that Joe was so like his mother, compassionate, kind and down to earth.

"You should be so proud of Joe you know, he's been an absolute godsend this summer – not sure how we'd have coped without him actually."

"I am proud of him, but I worry he's had to grow up too soon with his dad being absent a lot of the time. He's extremely fond of Beth, I know, but I worry about where this friendship is going, to be honest. They're too young to get in too deep, they're just kids really and Joe has to come home and return to school in a few weeks. I'm sure this time in Lincoln has been good for him too though, a spot of independence, albeit in a safe environment with you for back up, so huge thanks for that opportunity."

"No problem, none at all. Perhaps I could put your mind at rest a little though. I'm not with them all the time, of course, but I'm sure they're not …. you know …. sleeping together, if that's what you're worried about."

"No, not exactly, not just that, they've both reached the age of consent after all. Teenage urges are very strong though, we know that. No, it's more the emotional side of things; they need to experience other people, other boyfriends and girlfriends, before they get too bound up in each other. God, I've got to go through all this again, with Freddy, one day!" Joyce pondered Martha's words for a moment, before changing the subject.

"I wonder if you could fill me in on some of the details that I don't know, as you were on hand. Beth has told me all about the pregnancy and so forth and I know some of what happened to Ray's clinic, but not the details. It's like a jigsaw puzzle with pieces missing – would you mind?"

"Of course, you're Beth's family and I'm sure she's told you all that she knows. Joe also confided a lot in me last year, when he didn't know how to help Beth, so what do you want to know?" The two women chatted for a long time, until Joyce had a completely clear picture of all that had gone on with the abortion clinic, the unethical stem cell research and student programme, the medical negligence tribunal and Ray being effectively 'struck off,' the sale of their home too, the attack on Kate Monroe, the whole shebang.

"Wow, I never knew, incredible. The only missing piece is who Holly's actual father is, but I expect that's gone to the grave with Ray, we'll never know for sure and neither will she. Molly still believes it's Joe, but we all know it's not. I know it's someone who stayed at their house, Ray all but told me so. Perhaps Beth will work it out one day, when she's ready to, by a process of elimination, but for now she's happy so we should let sleeping dogs lie."

"I agree, cheers to that. Ooh, my glass is empty, is there any more in the bottle?"

"Absolutely, let's finish it off, we've earned it today."

#

SEPTEMBER

It was incredibly difficult for Beth, leaving Holly at the creche, the first time they'd been separated for more than an hour or two for nine months. Beth shed a few tears as she walked away from her baby crying in the arms of the nursery nurse, but she had to focus and face her first day as a student, starting her new course. It was a good day and she found it easy to make a few new friends, which was vital with Joe back living with his parents and back at school. Who knew when she'd see him again, maybe not until Christmas?

Joyce continued her work online, having interviews with clients via Zoom during the weekdays and returning to Dublin for just one weekend per month. She planned that this would continue until Gwen's situation resolved itself one way or another and was happy to resume some sort of normality with Beth and Holly. They'd begun meeting in the hospital cafeteria at around five-o-clock each weekday for a cuppa and a teacake, then each spending thirty minutes with Gwen and thirty minutes entertaining Holly before going home together for the evening. It was a good opportunity for them to catch up on each other's days and simultaneously switch off from their own.

It was on one such thirty-minute session, whilst Beth was reading the final sentences of Thornyhold to Gwen, that an unexpected corner was turned. It was the fourth time this story had been read to Gwen during her time horizontal in hospital, in the knowledge that it was her absolute favourite and in the hope that it would somehow reach through the fog of her unconsciousness. Beth could almost recite it from memory now, or at least parts of it.

'……...I overheard one of my grandchildren, turning the pages of my first illustrated herbal, say to her sister:

"You know, Jill, I sometimes think that Grandmother could have been a witch if she had wanted to." '

Beth closed the book and looked up at her own grandmother, only to discover a wide-awake pair of eyes looking at her. Beth waited and watched for the all too familiar stare to subside, with Gwen closing her eyes and disappearing into her silent world again, but the stare continued. Beth immediately took hold of Gwen's hand and held it for a moment when she heard a very raspy whisper:

"Lovely story, lovely."

"Gran, oh Gran, do you know who I am?"

"Beth, it's Beth," she managed with a very scratchy throat, then she closed her eyes again and drifted off to sleep with the merest hint of a smile on her face.

#

NOVEMBER

Holly and Gwen were both tucked up in their beds for the night, at the end of another busy day. Holly had taken her first proper steps at the creche that day and, sadly, Beth had missed them, but they'd been repeated during the evening, so Beth was happy. Gwen had been doing similar exercises at the physiotherapy department of the hospital, regaining strength in her legs and beginning to go for short walks without the need of a walking frame. Joyce and Beth were relaxing in front of the telly when Joyce muted it and approached a topic she'd been pondering for a couple of weeks.

"Beth, I've been thinking about something a lot lately and I want your opinion, so tell me what you think. Be honest with me – if you hate the idea just say so."

"OK, now I'm intrigued, what is it?"

"Well, the last twelve months have been an absolute whirlwind of change for us all, don't you think? I was wondering about getting it all down on paper."

"How do you mean, like a diary?"

"No, I mean a story. With your permission, I'd like to write a story, your story, our story. You know I'm a literary agent and novels are my world, so to speak. I've got loads of contacts, so it wouldn't be hard to do – maybe I'll get a ghost-writer or something, if actually writing isn't my strength, what do you think?"

"Um, well, I'm not against the idea, but would it be interesting enough? Would people want to read about me, us?"

"The way I see it, you had a really tough year last year and you came through it with flying colours. All our lives changed when you came to Lincoln and Holly was born, then Dad died. Everything that's happened since too, it's amazing, especially now that Mum is home and recovering well, when your dad wanted to consign her to an early grave. It would be a story about survival, about turning life around against difficult odds. You've told me so much of what happened to you and Martha filled in the gaps about what happened with your dad's clinic and everything, after you'd come here, so what do you think?"

"I think it's a lot to put into one book, so maybe do two? One about life and one about death?"

"Yes, good thinking. We can do two books. The first could be your experience and Holly's birth, then the second could be a message not to give up on people who are long-term ill in hospital and recognising the threats of euthanasia. I mean, look at Dad and your father, there was no saving them, but Mum's back here with us and doing great. If you're happy, I think we could do this Beth."

"Another thought Joyce, it would be a great keepsake for Holly, the full story of her first year of life and details which may get forgotten otherwise; she'd know the truth, the good as well as the painful bad, but that's life isn't it? What would you call the books?"

"Well, I think an excellent title for the first one would just be 'Beth,' plain and simple, unless you have any objections? No personal information regarding where you live, your full name and location or anything, just your Christian name. Is that alright?"

"Mmmm, OK and the second story?"

"Well, you're the catalyst, the person who came into our lives and turned them upside down in so many ways love. Don't get me wrong, my life has become sooo much fuller and more complete with you and Holly in it – you've become the daughter and granddaughter I never had, I love it. You've also given Mum a reason to carry on and shown her she has more time left to enjoy with you two in her life; you're both the reason she came back to us, I'm sure, because she'd all but given up for a while when Dad died. So, the second title should simply be 'Beth Again,' what do you think?"

"OK, if you're sure. Will these stories earn you any money?"

"Ah, I've thought about that too, partly after talking with Martha so much." Joyce's excitement was growing visibly and it was infectious – Beth was eager to hear more.

"What do you mean?"

"As I see it, if it hadn't been for Martha's beliefs and the advice and support she gave you, you may not have had Holly in your life. I'm not religious, you know that, but her faith and Joe's has influenced us all; also, everything that the doctors at the hospital said, when Ray was trying to end Mum's treatment and let her slide away, had a huge impact on me. They work so hard to preserve life when it's viable – sadly not your father's – they really are against euthanasia and assisted suicide, so I think we could help a bit if we earn anything from the books. I thought perhaps we could split the earnings, half to help support you and Holly over the coming months or years, half to the Pro-life organisation Martha works with. The Society for the Protection of Unborn Children fights to protect all vulnerable life, young and old, so what do you think?"

"Fabulous, I can't wait," then she got up and gave Joyce the biggest hug ever. "I'll go and get us a glass of wine to celebrate. Oooh, I'm going to be famous – maybe. *Beth* and *Beth Again*," then she skipped off to the kitchen in search of the wine and two glasses.

THE END

Useful Contact Details

www.nhs.uk/conditions/euthanasia-and-assisted-suicide
www.nhs.uk/conditions/end-of-life-care/
en.wikipedia.org/wiki/Euthanasia-in-the-United-Kingdom
www.politics.co.uk/reference/euthanasia

Pro-life resources dealing with end of life issues:
Care Not Killing – carenotkilling.org.uk
Dehydration Lifeline – dehydrationlifeline.org
Lives Worth Living –
www.spuc.org.uk/Get-Involved/Campaign/Lives-Worth-Living
SPUC Patients First Network – help for relatives and friends of
patients at immediate risk of euthanasia by dehydration and
starving: 020 7091 7091

Find Patient advice and liaison services (PALS) services - NHS
https://www.nhs.uk/service-search/other-services/   Patient-
advice-and-liaison-services-(PALS)/LocationSearch/363

Medical Defence Union
https://www.themdu.com/

School Age Mothers Programme:
www.education-ni.gov.uk/articles/school-age-mothers-
programme

Educational Welfare Services:
www.info.co.uk/search

16 to 19 Bursary Fund - GOV.UK
https://www.gov.uk/1619-bursary-fund

Jumperoo – Fisher-Price - £51 - £119 (approx.) at time of printing
– Amazon

'Thornyhold' By Mary Stewart available from Amazon

Acknowledgements

Once again, my heartfelt thanks must go to a small group of invaluable people for their time, support and positive response to my second story. I could not have done it without you all.

Ian, for being so emotional about a topic which is close to his heart – your tears at the story meant more than you will ever know.

Dear friends Jesse and Clare Lawrence and Jan Taylor for, once again, giving so generously of their time and not being scared to offer much needed constructive criticisms – your opinions have added greatly to my story.

My ex-GP Mark Hedges M.B., Ch.B. for overseeing medical correctness again – your professionalism and amazing bedside manner saw our family through three decades and now, years later, your help with my books has been wonderful, thank you.

Finally, Saskia at New Generation Publishing, for patiently guiding me through the minefield of publishing a book, many thanks.

Discussion Questions

- On Page 8, Molly and Ray's holiday is described as *'living a selfish lie of wine, food, sea and decadence'* – why?
- Why do you think Gwen leaves her house to Beth in her will instead of her own two children?
- Do you think this decision creates unnecessary problems for Beth?
- Does Gwen understand the true natures of her two children?
- How do you think you would react to inheriting a house aged eighteen?
- What makes Molly and Ray such poor parents?
- Do you think poor parenting can be inherited?
- Is Beth justified in keeping her relationship with Joe virtually platonic?
- Is Joe unrealistically patient with Beth?
- Do you think Beth is honest about her true feelings or just confused?
- Do you think Ray deserves what happens to him?
- Is your understanding of the differences between euthanasia, passive euthanasia and assisted suicide clearer having read ***Beth Again***?
- Has your opinion about these subjects changed having read the story?

Lightning Source UK Ltd.
Milton Keynes UK
UKHW010626110921
390346UK00001B/71

9 781800 313460